Stranger alert.

Arianna fumbled around on the table until she located one of the many whistles they owned underneath her napkin. They had rehearsed this plan numerous times, never expecting to carry it out. She sucked in a deep breath and issued the shrill warning that quickly brought Simon to his feet.

The seven-year-old stood there looking like David coming up against Goliath. Ari considered his options, wondering if he could make it to the stairs before the intruder came too close.

Where was Tom? Had this man overpowered him elsewhere on the property? Ari ran to the door and banged on the glass. Nana hurried over. She pointed, and the woman picked up the phone. Ari started down the stairs, praying God would deliver them safely from this man.

Noting the commotion, the stranger drew to a halt. He lifted his hands and yelled, "I'm with Bishop Security!"

TERRY FOWLER is a native Tarheel who loves calling coastal North Carolina home. Single, she works full-time and is active in her small church. Her greatest pleasure comes from the way God has used her writing to share His message. Her hobbies include gardening, crafts, and genealogical research. Terry invites everyone to visit her web page at terryfowler.net.

Books by Terry Fowler

Don't miss out on any of our super romances. Write to us at the following address for information on our newest releases and club information.

Heartsong Presents Readers' Service
PO Box 721
Uhrichsville, OH 44683

Or visit www.heartsongpresents.com

With Not a Spoken Word

Terry Fowler

Heartsong Presents

To Jesus Christ—the one protector we can always depend on.

To Mary, Tammy, JoAnne, Rachel, and Margie—thanks for helping me make my stories work.

A note from the Author:
I love to hear from my readers! You may correspond with me by writing:

Terry Fowler
Author Relations
PO Box 721
Uhrichsville, OH 44683

ISBN 978-1-61626-373-7

WITH NOT A SPOKEN WORD

Our mission is to publish and distribute inspirational products offering exceptional value and biblical encouragement to the masses.

PRINTED IN THE U.S.A.

one

Arianna Kent sat on a deck perched on the side of a mountain and thought about living high in the sky. Unlike her parents' Gold Coast penthouse with its sky top terraces and incredible vistas of the lake and the Chicago skyline, this place seemed more like a tree house.

Surrounded by thick forests of trees to her right and left, scenic Lake Hiwassee stretched out before her as far as the eye could see. In the distance, other houses looked down from their high perches with long flights of stairs leading down to the lake. Though the day was early, the August sun made itself felt as it sparkled off the silvery gray water. She pushed away the remnants of her breakfast and shifted her gaze to the floating dock where Simon played. He knelt too close to the edge, and she wanted to call out to him to take care but remained silent, frustrated by her inability to speak the words of warning that churned inside her head.

How could she protect her younger brother when she couldn't even warn him of danger? Maybe she should turn his care over to someone else until she got her voice back. She grimaced at the thought.

Ari wasn't about to abandon Simon when he needed her most. He'd spent far too much of his young life being cared for by someone other than his family. She also needed to get past the self-pity. She wasn't alone. Elsewhere on the property, Tom Brown, her father's longtime chauffeur and now their self-appointed security guard, patrolled the area with a dedication that couldn't be bought. He had worked around the clock, determined to keep them safe.

Their elderly nanny, Dora Etheridge, had stepped up to the role of parent pro tem out of love for the charges she often referred to as her babies.

Still, with her inability to speak, Nana's age, and only Tom providing security, there was no way they could hope to protect Simon from every threat that might arise. And while Gary Bishop of Bishop Security insisted they were secure here in this Murphy, North Carolina, safe house, Arianna found it impossible to feel safe anywhere.

As a Christian, Ari believed God would care for them, but her human side had brought her here. She willingly accepted this safe haven in hopes of overcoming her sudden disability but couldn't relinquish the anxiety and terror that kept her awake at night or the overwhelming dread that never went away.

They hadn't wanted to leave their home and lives behind, but their emotional response to the idea that they were not safe in Chicago gave them sufficient motivation to run away.

They'd flown into the Western Carolina Regional Airport on Tuesday, picked up the SUV Gary arranged, loaded their belongings inside, and took off for the address Tom had been given. As he followed the GPS instructions that led them along the rural roads to the Bear Paw community, Ari couldn't begin to imagine where they were going. At best she considered they would be staying in a log cabin in the middle of nowhere.

The gorgeous home was indeed a type of log cabin, but its open design and ample interior space had been a pleasant surprise. The gated community gave her a degree of comfort; so did the fact that the two houses, one for them and the other for security, were located in a paved clearing at the end of their own street, the surrounding wooded area too overgrown to be easily negotiated. The area seemed isolated but wasn't. People surrounded them in the mountaintop houses situated throughout the wooded area, and yet each home had its own private access from the paved streets that wound throughout the community.

The spectacular view appealed to her senses, and the house provided them with the privacy they required. Ari needed to believe that no one would find them here.

She stood and moved to the railing. Simon glanced up and yelled for her to come on down. Ari shook her head. She held up both hands and gestured toward herself, hoping he would understand her sign language. Simon took a couple of steps toward the center of the dock, and Ari flashed him a big smile and a thumbs-up.

She returned to the table. Her staff meeting would begin soon. Ari signed on to her laptop and then jotted a few thoughts on a legal pad in preparation for the long-distance event. The Chicago Hotel Kent would continue to function in her absence. Its guests would come and go, hopefully happy and content with their stays, unaware the grieving manager conducted business from a deck hundreds of miles away in the Great Smoky Mountains.

That didn't make it any easier to accept that she couldn't be there, doing the work she enjoyed and living the life she'd created for herself. Never the type to sit around wasting time, Ari hated feeling useless. There was so much more she could be doing in Chicago, but for now she had to be content here. Simon's life could depend on her doing the right thing.

From the corner of her eye, movement and a flash of color on the hill alongside the house caught Ari's attention. She jerked around and spotted a man strolling down the pathway.

Stranger alert.

Arianna fumbled around on the table until she located one of the many whistles they owned underneath her napkin. They had rehearsed this plan numerous times, never expecting to carry it out. She sucked in a deep breath and issued the shrill warning that quickly brought Simon to his feet.

The seven-year-old stood there looking like David coming up against Goliath. Ari considered his options, wondering if he could make it to the stairs before the intruder came too close.

Where was Tom? Had this man overpowered him elsewhere on the property? Ari ran to the door and banged on the glass. Nana hurried over. She pointed, and the woman picked up the phone. Ari started down the stairs, praying God would deliver them safely from this man.

Noting the commotion, the stranger drew to a halt. He lifted his hands and yelled, "I'm with Bishop Security! My name is Mitchell Ellis." He pulled a badge from his pocket and flung it in Simon's direction.

The child took a few steps forward, not taking his eyes off the intruder as he bent to pick it up. He edged back toward safety before he checked it out. "It's a Bishop badge," Simon called to his sister.

The breath rushed from Ari, and she grabbed hold of the stair railing to support herself as her knees weakened. Why hadn't she thought of that earlier? Gary had planned to send another man to help Tom as soon as he could make the arrangements. She hadn't expected him to arrive without some type of advance warning.

Where was Tom? Why hadn't he alerted them to the man's arrival? Surely the guardhouse had notified him.

Nana stepped out on the deck and announced, "Tom says it's the Bishop guy."

At the same time, the man named Mitchell shouted up to her. "I spoke with Tom Brown. Told him I would introduce myself. I thought Gary had told you I'd be arriving this afternoon."

"You can come on up," Simon invited as he returned the badge.

The two of them moved toward the stairs. Simon laughed at something the man said. Ari returned to the deck and sat down at the table, fearful her legs would give way.

The climb to the deck took longer for the man. He paused to draw in several deep breaths before he managed, "I am sorry, Ms. Kent. I saw Simon on the dock and thought I'd introduce myself. I should have realized you were on high alert."

"Mitch said it's a good thing you didn't have a gun or he'd probably be dead," Simon told her.

Ari forced a smile. He probably meant it as a joke, but considering how threatened she'd felt, "shoot first, ask questions later" might have been her initial reaction.

"You okay, Ari?" Simon asked, grabbing her hand.

She forced another smile, determined to hide her inner agitation from them. Her gaze came back to Mitchell Ellis. This man looked nothing like she expected. Most of the Bishop men blended into the background, but this was not a man who faded into obscurity.

Ari found herself acutely conscious of his tall, muscular physique. He wore the expensive clothing with the air of a man who knew he looked good. Not that there was anything wrong with that. She found his aristocratic facial features, olive complexion, and perfectly cut dark brown hair to be very attractive as well. His eyes were the same shade of brown as her favorite dark chocolate. He reached out to shake her hand, and she noted his hand was that of an executive, the clean nails buffed to a shine. She estimated him to be in his midthirties.

Stop being so critical, she chided. So the man took care of himself. There was nothing wrong with being well groomed and immaculately turned out when meeting a new client.

Arianna focused on Simon's chatter. Her heart thudded in an uneven rhythm that matched her breathing. Though she believed Mitchell Ellis meant them no harm, the reality lingered in her thoughts.

And the episode pointed out one more chink in their security system. She hadn't been able to reach Tom, and where would Simon have gone if the man had been a predator?

His options—a long flight of stairs, the heavily wooded area, and the lake—weren't really possibilities. A grown man could have easily overcome the child in any of those places. She needed to contact Gary Bishop. Maybe even insist on full-time armed bodyguards to protect Simon when he played outside the house.

Her computer screen caught her attention, reminding Ari that a conference room of managers waited for her to join the meeting. She pointed to the laptop and turned her attention to the business at hand.

❧

Stupid! Stupid! Stupid! Mitchell Ellis berated himself. Brother-in-law or not, Gary would tell him to get lost fast if he pulled another stunt like this.

What had he been thinking? He should have known better than to come up at any point other than the front door. They were afraid and had every right to feel threatened by a stranger strolling casually down the hillside.

But he'd become so used to walking along the path to the dock during his vacations that it never occurred to him that it wasn't a good idea. He'd been considered a decent security man in his day. Had the years of medical school and working with patients dulled his edge? Anyone with Security 101 knew you didn't scare a client like that.

Awareness flowed to life within him when he caught Arianna Kent watching him. Earlier when he'd looked up and seen her beautiful face in distress, Mitch wished he could rewind and approach them correctly. Her reserved smile and the way she hurriedly shifted her green gaze back to the computer screen gave him pause. Surely this beauty wasn't shy.

When Gary had approached him regarding the use of his two somewhat secluded Murphy mountain homes in the gated community of Bear Paw, he insisted they could easily hide the Kents there.

Today's security breach showed a hole in his theory. Mitch had witnessed their fright as they considered what to do. Simon had nowhere to run and Arianna had no way to help him, untenable situations for them both.

"Come on, Mitch," Simon said as he opened the door off the deck. "I'll introduce you to Nana while Ari has her meeting. She'll give us something cold to drink. You think it's always this mad hot here?"

"It is summer."

Mitch glanced back at the young woman he'd rarely seen in the Chicago social columns. Petite and slim, she wore white shorts and a royal-blue sleeveless top. She'd pulled her white-blond hair up into a loose chignon with little tendrils framing her ivory-skinned heart-shaped face. Fragile. The one word summed her up perfectly.

From the rumors, Arianna Kent had gone off to college and found God. Some socialites snickered because she preferred church to parties, but Mitch hoped Arianna's decision gave her great joy. Especially at a time like this when she had experienced so much pain.

"You coming?" Simon asked.

Arianna looked up again, this time her gaze bolder and more confident when their eyes met. He smiled, tossed a wave in her direction, and said, "Right behind you."

❧

Ari felt his gaze on her and assumed he was analyzing her reaction to his sudden shocking appearance. She doubted he wanted to get into trouble with the new boss on his first day.

The computer chimed as her staff indicated their presence in the room. Ari laughed at their aliases. Captain Cook. Big Money. Broom Hilda. They were truly getting into the intrigue.

Shannon Crown, aka Princess and Ari's assistant general manager, had already sent the agenda and daily operation update that morning.

Ari couldn't imagine a more dedicated employee. Her friend's exceptional work ethic inspired Ari. Having Shannon there was as good as being there in person. They had met in college when Shannon became her roomie and later led her to Christ.

After graduation, Ari suggested her friend come to Chicago and talk to her father about a job. Shannon had worked her way through college part-time in a hotel sales office. Within months of starting work at Hotel Kent, her impressive sales ability garnered Charles Kent's attention, and he offered her the position of sales manager. Ari had found Shannon's guilt over receiving a management position humorous.

"I should be working my way up with you," she insisted.

Charles Kent believed Ari needed to learn the business from the ground up, and her first job assignment was as a front desk clerk.

"No way," Ari denied. "I was born into a family of hoteliers and you have more experience than me."

From his corporate office, her father knew exactly how Ari performed. Determined to prove herself, Arianna mastered each aspect of operations in a very short time. No one could refer to her as the spoiled child of the owner. She worked shoulder to shoulder with the other employees. Within a year, her father put Arianna in charge.

Ari had managed the hotel for three years now, maintaining the high level of operation that resulted in award-winning recognition. She asked nothing of her staff she wasn't willing to give and received their dedication in return.

Time to get their meeting under way. Ari typed, *Good morning.*

At her request, Gary had directed his IT people to set up a private chat room on the Bishop Security site so they could communicate using a question-and-answer session.

Old-fashioned, considering the technology used by most businesses, but no one knew where they were and Ari planned to keep it that way. She had an air card that was not traceable to her or the company, a disposable phone well stocked with minutes, and no video cams. No reason since no one needed to see her mute persona on a screen.

In turn, each manager reported on their respective area of operation, covering the problems and plans for sales, food and beverage, front desk operations, housekeeping, and accounting. They discussed the situations every hotel dealt with in the course of providing quality services to their guests and even the unique things that at times baffled them all. They reviewed upcoming events and ways to increase their revenue in a difficult economic time. Fortunately for them, the hotel chain was popular with tourists and businesspeople.

Almost an hour later, Ari concluded the meeting, thanking each of them for their efforts on her behalf. Several additional messages appeared, asking if she and Simon were doing okay. Teary-eyed, she assured them they were doing as well as could be expected.

Grief was a strange thing. She would be fine, and then a random memory triggered the pain and she cried for hours. Losing her parents naturally would have been difficult enough, but finding them murdered was at times more than she could bear.

Her cell beeped and Ari found a text message from Gary

Bishop. One of her conditions for hiring his firm had been that she be able to contact him at any time, day or night. She paid his firm very well to guarantee every aspect of their safety and didn't feel this was an unrealistic request.

She read, HERE'S A PHOTO OF THE NEW GUY. MITCHELL ELLIS WILL BE A GREAT ADDITION TO YOUR SECURITY TEAM.

A little late, Ari thought. She typed a response. THANKS, GARY. HE ARRIVED UNEXPECTEDLY OVER AN HOUR AGO. WILL DISCUSS THE DRAMA THAT OCCURRED IN GREATER DETAIL AFTER REVIEWING THE INCIDENT WITH MR. ELLIS. PROBABILITY WE MAY NEED TO TAKE FURTHER SECURITY PRECAUTIONS.

Gary immediately texted that he would be waiting to hear back from her.

Ari closed the lid on the laptop, leaving it on the table. There was other work, but it could wait. Digging around on the cluttered tabletop, she found the white dry-erase board and a marker. Yet another of the outdated tools she used for communication these days.

two

Inside, Mitch and Simon were seated at the table drinking soda. Ari pulled out a chair. She scribbled busily on the whiteboard, hoping he could read her writing. *"Gary sent a photo. Told him you'd already arrived with ensuing drama."*

Looking sheepish, Mitch said, "Sorry, Ms. Kent."

"Call me Ari. It concerns me that you slipped up on us like that," she wrote. *"If I hadn't seen the movement, you could have gotten to Simon rather quickly. How do you recommend we avoid that in the future?"*

The wait was prolonged as he drank from the glass and considered his response. Ari thought of the question as a test. Wrong answer, he failed and she would send him packing no matter how confident Gary felt.

Mitch lowered the glass to the table, taking even longer to center it on the coaster. "We've been talking." He waved his hand to indicate Simon and himself. "Simon understands that he needs to think about where he is at all times and where he can go if a stranger appears."

"He says if there are no options, I shouldn't be there," Simon piped up. "I won't be able to leave the house."

Mitch spoke with quiet emphasis, glancing at the boy as he spoke. "I'm fairly certain most people who come to visit wouldn't come down that steep slope."

"We don't have visitors," Simon muttered.

His comment gave Ari pause. Not that she claimed to be an expert on seven-year-old boys, but she did understand that he missed his home and friends as much as she did. Ari wanted this to be over for both their sakes.

"Someone with the intent to kill might very well choose that route," Ari wrote.

She angled the board about so that Mitch could read what she'd written.

He shrugged and said, "I doubt they'd exert themselves to that extent."

Ari considered his unspoken implication. Anyone could use a rifle to pick them off like bugs on a leaf. There were too many perfect hiding places among the hills and trees.

Mitch continued, "I've been thinking and plan to make recommendations to Gary. We could install a screen to block access, but I think our best course of action is to place alarms that give you adequate time to react."

Ari considered both ideas. While the screen would keep them from view when they were down near the water, it would also keep them from being seen by the occupants of the security house.

"Why can't we go home?" Simon asked.

She wiped the board clean and wrote, *"You know why."*

"I could look out for you and Nana," Simon said. "There's nothing to do here."

Ari stared into his green eyes—their father's eyes. She wanted to tousle his blond hair and tell him everything would be okay, but she couldn't make that promise. She had to protect him even if he came to hate her for doing so. She loved Simon far too much to ever allow something bad to happen to him.

Besides, she'd seen to it that he had plenty to keep him busy. They had turned the entire lower level into a game room complete with television, game console, pinball machine, piles of his favorite books, trading cards, action figures, not to mention board games, boxes of science projects, and Legos.

"Do you understand why you're here, Simon?" Mitch asked.

Idly pushing his glass around on the table, he nodded.

"Why can't they find the people who killed Mom and Dad? It's been forever."

Ari understood that a week could seem like a long time to a seven-year-old.

"The police are doing everything they can," Mitch said. "Gary has been in touch with the Chicago PD and says they are under a lot of pressure to solve the case."

"I hope they do it soon," Simon said, his vexation evident. "I want to go home."

"There's more to this than finding the killer," Mitch said. "Your sister has suffered a traumatic shock and needs this time to recover."

The boy stood and threw an arm around her shoulders. "I'm sorry, Ari."

She kissed his cheek and mouthed, *Love you, Simon.*

"Love you back. Can I go play?"

Ari nodded.

"See you, Mitch." He ran off down the stairs.

Ari wrote, *"Please don't make him feel guilty over what's happened to me. The situation is bad enough without that. He's entitled to feel restless. I've ripped him away from everything he's ever known and brought him to the middle of nowhere."*

Determination highlighted his handsome features. "He needs to understand you're doing this for him. It might make him think twice before taking a chance that could cost him his life."

His comment surprised her. She'd expected him to say, "Yes, ma'am," and go on with business, not challenge her. She cleaned the board and wrote, *"He's a child. Our responsibility is to protect him. What about an armed guard?"*

Mitch shook his head. "I don't care for guns around children. Bad things happen when weapons are in the mix. We can find less dangerous ways to protect you both." His gaze focused directly on her. "I apologize for frightening you unnecessarily. Your response was excellent. Whistles, air horns, anything that makes noise can be an excellent deterrent."

An image of them tooting noisemakers as they ran away from the killer immediately came to mind. It seemed almost too silly to imagine, but Ari agreed that guns could be hazardous.

She scribbled on the board and held it up. *"Why didn't Gary come with you?"*

Mitch grimaced and said, "He's tied up in the city. I told him I could handle the introduction on my own. He gave me an overview of the case and instructions on how to handle the job. It's a very private area. The guard at the gate isn't going to tell anyone you're here, nor will he allow anyone access. The dense woods surrounding the house will also provide a level of protection. Not many people would brave those hilly woods to get to this point."

"Not many people would access a penthouse apartment either," she wrote.

He nodded agreement, his expressive face showing his sympathy. Few Chicagoans had missed the report of the Kents' murder. Every major news outlet to the national level had covered the story. The hoteliers had been well known throughout the United States. One of few remaining family-owned chains, the Kent Hotels were popular.

"After we finish here, I plan to walk the perimeter. Then I'll talk with Gary. Is there anything else you need me to do now that I've arrived?"

Ari shook her head.

Nana placed a salad plate with fruit and baked chicken on the table before her and commanded, "Eat."

Ari glanced at her watch and saw that the morning had disappeared and it was indeed lunchtime. Her appetite had been almost nonexistent since the night her parents were killed. Nana seemed equally determined that she would not fade away in her grief.

The woman served Mitch and placed a basket of croissants and yeast rolls along with honey butter on the table. She walked over to the stairs and called Simon. He bounded into the room and took his place at the dining table. Nana set a club sandwich and fries before him. She brought her fruit salad over and sat down.

"Let's join hands and say grace," she said, reaching out to Ari and Simon. Simon reached for Mitch's hand. Nana thanked the Lord for His provisions and for Mitch's presence to help keep them safe.

One positive of this place was the lack of formality, Ari thought as she forked a piece of apple into her mouth. At the penthouse, Nana would have taken her meal in the kitchen or nursery. Ari liked sharing the table with her.

Ari sneaked one of Simon's fries.

"Hey," he cried, moving his plate out of reach.

She grinned and poked him playfully.

Simon giggled and blocked her attempts to snag more with his small body.

"If you want fries, Ari, there's more on the counter."

Ari retrieved the plate, pausing to take the ketchup bottle from the fridge. She slid the plate in Mitch's direction.

He took one and popped it into his mouth. "French fries are hard to resist."

"I'd have made more, but we're out of potatoes," Nana said. "I need to take a trip into Murphy."

"Is it something I can do for you?" Mitch asked with a pleasant smile.

"Groceries."

"Give me a list and I'll have them picked up."

Good luck with that one, Ari thought. Ever since she'd taken on the self-appointed role of cook here in the mountains,

Nana hadn't trusted her shopping to anyone.

"No thank you. I prefer to choose my own meat and produce."

"Then one of us will take you. I'm covering the day shift, but Tom can drive you later this afternoon after he wakes."

Ari grabbed her marker and wrote, *Let's all go. I wouldn't mind getting away from here for a bit.*

Mitch frowned. "That could be dangerous. It's difficult to protect three people in a public place."

"We look out for each other," Nana said. "Ari and Simon have been in my care ever since they were born. I'm not about to let anyone harm either of them."

"When did you want to go?"

"In the morning will be fine. Today is nearly over."

Ari nearly laughed at Nana's timekeeping. It was noon, not midnight. The phone next to her plate beeped.

"Please turn that off," Nana ordered. "Can't have a decent meal without some kind of technology interrupting."

Ari slid the phone around to read the e-mail. She felt the oncoming tears and hurriedly wrote, *"Excuse me,"* on the whiteboard.

※

"What happened? Is something wrong?" Mitch asked when she disappeared into the bedroom off the left of the main room.

Nana reached for the phone and read the message. She frowned and laid it back on the tabletop. "I'd better check on her."

Mitch looked at Simon, who didn't appear the least concerned by the drama. He continued to work his way through the french fries as if nothing had happened. He glanced toward the door where the women had disappeared, not sure what he should do. He looked back at Simon and found the boy watching him as he ate. "Have you been fishing since you arrived?"

Simon used a paper napkin to clean his fingers. "I don't know how."

"Not much to it," Mitch said. "Stick some bait on the hook and wait for the fish to decide he wants a snack."

Simon frowned. "What's fun about that?"

Mitch chuckled. "It's the challenge. Man against nature. You fish to catch the big one that makes all your friends jealous. Then you mount that fish and hang it on the wall. They have to catch a bigger fish.

"And then you need to learn how to tell fish tales about the one that got away." He indicated how men usually measured their catch.

"Take me fishing and I'll catch one this big." Simon jumped up and threw both arms open wide.

Mitch laughed at the boy's antics. "Well buddy, you've got that part down. You really know how to exaggerate."

Simon's childish laughter filled the room. The women returned just as Simon jumped up. Nana told him to sit down and finish his meal.

"Ari received a reminder to check on the reservations for tomorrow night. She'd planned a surprise party for her dad's birthday," Nana explained softly as they sat down.

Mitch grimaced in sympathy. He could see Ari had been crying and wondered if his presence had been her reason for returning to the dining table. Perhaps he should make himself scarce.

"Can Mitch take me fishing?"

Too late, Mitch thought as he noted the way Ari's attention moved from the salad she rearranged to the boy and then to him. He'd have to stay and answer any questions she might have.

"He says it's real easy."

She reached for her whiteboard. *"We'll discuss this later."*

"Please, Ari."

She tapped the message on the board with her marker.

"Okay," he mumbled and turned his attention back to his lunch.

"I have fishing gear at the house," Mitch said. "I'd make sure he's safe."

Her gaze fixed on him as she tapped the dry-erase board a second time.

She wiped the board and wrote, *"Shannon said she sent you a couple of new games. We'll pick them up when we go into town."*

"Okay," Simon declared almost happily.

They finished their lunch in silence. Mitch was the first to speak.

"I need to get to work. Simon, would you mind showing me around downstairs? Thanks for lunch," Mitch told Nana. "It was delicious."

three

Ari lay in her bed, listening to the house settle for the night. Simon and Nana slept, but she remained wide-awake, considering everything that had transpired that day. She'd refused the prescription the doctor offered, not wanting to medicate herself to the point that she might not be aware if something happened outside the house.

She tossed and turned until the sheet tangled hopelessly with her long cotton nightgown around her legs. Fighting free of the covers, Ari slid off the bed and padded barefoot to the door. Silence. Nana slept in the bedroom on the opposite side of the open kitchen, dining, and living room area. Simon slept on the sofa bed in the sunroom. He couldn't understand why he couldn't sleep in one of the two downstairs bedrooms, but Ari wanted him where she could get to him quickly.

She pulled on a sweater to protect herself against the night chill and slipped through the house and out the french door onto the deck. Ari chose a rocker at the end near her bedroom, not wanting to disturb Simon's sleep. She felt the cool dampness of the dew as she sat down and pulled her feet up onto the curved seat, jerking the flowing cotton gown over her legs.

Should she have said yes to Simon's pleas to go fishing with Mitchell Ellis? Her brother had wrapped her around his tiny fingers almost from birth, and Ari knew he wasn't about to stop now. She hadn't wanted to disappoint the child but needed to get to know Mitchell Ellis better before trusting him completely with Simon. She knew nothing more than what Gary had shared, and while his confidence should have been sufficient to calm her nerves, it wasn't.

Once her eyes adjusted to the darkness, Ari appreciated the solitude. Peaceful. No twenty-four hours of people or traffic here. A new moon and very few stars in the sky tonight. In the distance she could see lights in homes where others remained awake. While she appreciated the sense of isolation the area generated, Ari knew there were people in the homes sprinkled throughout the mountain forest.

Every little sound, mostly scrambling wildlife and birds, drew Ari's focus. At times she imagined footsteps and froze until she decided it must be her imagination. Occasional breezes soughed through the trees, rustling leaves. The air smelled fresh and clean.

She took her phone from her pocket and checked her e-mail, seeing the reminder message that had appeared that day. Her father's birthday—the first of those she'd never celebrate with him. He would have been fifty-two. Much too young to die.

Ari read the e-mails through teary eyes, mostly invitations for charity fund-raisers. Didn't they understand that she was grieving? She wanted to blast them for their insensitivity. Instead she instructed Shannon to send the standard message. As long as things remained like this, there would be rare public appearances—no parties, no social engagements, and no church.

She closed her eyes to the nightmare image that filled her head every time she recalled that night.

"Call the police. My parents are dead." Gus, the doorman at her parents' home, heard her last spoken words.

She and Simon had spent their Saturday at a church function. Then she'd taken him and his friends out for pizza and a movie afterward, and it was around 11:00 p.m. when they arrived back at the penthouse. Ari promised to pick him up for church the next morning and sent him off to prepare for bed. She paused by her parents' bedroom door, intending to wish them a good night. The television volume seemed unusually loud, and Ari thought maybe they hadn't heard when there was no response to her knock.

She turned the knob and stuck her head around the open door. Inside, the bedside lamps glowed brightly, highlighting the carnage that had been wrought. Her parents lay still on the bed, their lifeblood seeping from their multiple stab wounds. Recalling the vast amount of bright red against the white bed linens still made her shiver. Ari knew without doubt that they were dead. No one could have survived such a vicious attack.

The screams came from deep down inside as she charged back into the hallway. Simon came running, asking what was wrong. Some part of her registered that he couldn't witness the nightmare in that room. She grabbed the boy and shoved him toward the private elevator they had arrived in minutes before.

"Ari, I'm wearing my pajamas," Simon objected, looking at his sister like she'd lost her mind.

She registered the superhero on his shirt and said, "We have to get out of here. Now."

In the lobby they ran to the desk. She spoke those final words in a state of disbelief, realizing too late that she shouldn't have said them in front of the child.

Simon's eyes widened, questioning her. "Ari?"

She nodded and Simon's pitiful wail broke her heart. She dropped to her knees and pulled him close, rocking him as they sobbed together. She wanted to comfort him, but the words would not come. The doorman guided them to a nearby sofa before notifying the police.

"Did someone really hurt Mom and Dad? Ari?" Simon looked at her questioningly. "You're scaring me. Why won't you say something?"

The question was a stab in her own heart. She worked her mouth, but nothing came out. Simon's cries started up again. She pulled her cell phone from her purse and typed, *"Can't talk. Call Nana."* She located the number and handed him the phone.

Their nanny had the night off. Her family was in town, and she planned to stay over at the hotel with her sister. Ari had made the arrangements herself.

"Nana," Simon said, his voice wobbly with emotion, "something's wrong with Ari. She can't talk. She told Gus Mom and Dad are dead." He paused to listen. "Okay."

He shoved the phone at Ari. "Nana wants to talk to you." She listened as the woman said she'd be right there.

"Ms. Kent? Are you okay? Can I do anything to help?"

She looked at Gus and shook her head. He had worked as a doorman since she was a child.

The image from the bedroom played over and over again in her head. Simon clung to her and Ari held on tight, her gaze moving around the lobby, fearful the killer or killers might have stuck around to finish the job.

The police arrived and the detective flashed his badge. "Can you tell us what happened?"

"She can't talk." Simon started to cry again. Ari pulled him into her lap.

A kindly female officer knelt by Ari's side, talking softly. "Is there anyone you'd like to call?"

"We called our Nana," Simon said with a mighty sniff.

"Okay. What's her name?"

The male detective produced a pen and paper. "We need you to share what happened."

As Ari wrote quickly, describing the scene she'd discovered upstairs in her parents' bedroom, the lobby filled with police and curious tenants.

"Is there somewhere private they can go?" the detective

asked, and the doorman led them to a small office.

"So you saw nothing?" the female officer asked.

Ari opened her mouth and still no words came out. "You need to go to the hospital," the woman said.

Ari wrote her family doctor's name and *"No hospital,"* underscoring the words three times.

Minutes later Nana arrived and convinced them to let her see the Kents. Both were in need of comfort and they sat on each side of the elderly woman.

The night stretched on into the predawn as the police worked the scene of the double homicide. The crime scene investigators arrived around the same time as Dr. Dwayne Graves.

His insistence that Ari go to the hospital so they could run tests met her refusal. She wrote that she was fine, but Dr. Graves insisted she was in shock.

Ari and Simon sat on the sofa while the crime scene techs fingerprinted them. She hugged him close as his tiny body trembled with sobs.

"When can they leave?" Nana asked the officer.

"Is there someplace safe they can go?"

"My place," Ari scribbled on the pad of paper.

Nana shook her head. "Not without protection." She called Tom Brown. He arrived within minutes and was brought into the office.

Keeping his voice low, Tom said, "We can't risk them getting to you or Simon. We need more security."

"We can put a car out front," the detective said.

They all agreed that would work for now.

On the way to her place, she texted Gary Bishop on the private cell number he'd given her. She'd met him a couple of times at the hotel when someone had hired him for security and felt comfortable with Bishop Security.

He arrived at the townhouse minutes after they did. After hearing what had happened, Gary immediately suggested they consider leaving Chicago for a while. Ari wouldn't feel safe in either of the family's Aspen and Greece vacation homes. Too many people knew of their existence. Gary promised to find them a place where they could feel secure.

The investigation and memorial service had delayed their departure, but Gary had carried through on his promise and now he'd sent someone to help keep them safe. Mitchell Ellis filled her head. Something about him didn't fit her image of a security man. Granted, her heart had beat a little faster after his arrival, but Ari couldn't say whether it was the man or her reaction to him that scared her nearly senseless.

❧

Late that night, Mitch patrolled the property and stayed out of range of the security lights, not wanting to frighten the family with the burst of bright lights Tom had warned him about. His was the only human presence in the area. Night-vision goggles enabled him to find his way without a flashlight.

Mitch had flown out of Chicago early that morning. Last weekend, his plan had been to work through his patient load and start his three-week vacation here in the mountains on Friday. Then Gary had called about using the two properties as safe houses for the Kents.

"I promised to find her a safe haven."

Mitch pointed out that the gated community with a guard had a good amount of traffic and wasn't totally private.

"Yeah, but the houses are blocked under your name, and providing extra security would make the situation workable. Ari's so freaked out right now that it's playing havoc with her condition."

Gary went on to share his concerns about putting them out there with a stranger and how glad he was that Tom Brown intended to go with or without his permission. He went on to outline Tom's experience.

"You'd have been foolish to refuse his help," Mitch observed.

This wasn't the first time he'd heard Arianna Kent's name. Dwayne Graves had called on Sunday afternoon for a consult. Mitch was no expert, but he had studied conversion disorder and knew that the affected part of the body had symbolic meaning whereby the conflict was converted into a physical symptom, which in Ari's case was her inability to talk. He'd told Dwayne to give it time.

Mitch knew what he had to do. He could see to it personally that Arianna Kent got the privacy and time she needed. When he volunteered to work security during his vacation, Gary was surprised but not about to say no to the perfect solution to his dilemma. Though Gary explained the Kents were willing to pay expenses, he would have offered his houses free of charge.

Mitch felt a strange mixture of sympathy and empathy for them. He knew about having your parents ripped from you. He particularly wanted them to feel safe during this time of grief. And while he looked out for them, he could see Arianna Kent's condition for himself.

Earlier that afternoon Mitch had called Gary to discuss the panic his arrival had caused.

"Since our client can afford it, we'll put technology to work for us," Gary said without hesitation. "I want them to feel safe. Are you okay with us adding a perimeter alarm on the driveway with a computer connection so we can see who is out there? And extending the alarm on the hill around the base of the house to include the stairs and the dock?"

"Do you think there's any chance they were followed? That someone could know where they are?"

"We're operating in the dark here. The police are no closer to learning who killed the Kents than they were on Saturday."

Mitch doodled on the notepad lying on the table. "So we protect them by land and by sea?"

"Right. I'll check into having alerts sent to your cell phones."

"Ari suggested an armed guard for Simon while he's outside playing. I don't like the idea."

"What brought that up?" Suspicion tinged Gary's question.

Mitch hesitated and then admitted, "My surprise appearance and subsequent discussion regarding them being aware of their surroundings. Things evolved when I said I didn't think anyone coming after them would bother to walk down the hill."

"Mitch, I didn't send you there to frighten my client more." He'd heard that same displeased huff of agitation when his brother-in-law was upset with his wife.

"She came up with the shooter idea on her own," Mitch defended.

Gary sighed again. "They probably shouldn't be out in the open during the day."

"You can't keep them locked up inside," Mitch protested. "That's no life for anyone."

"I know. But Ari has stressed that I should spare no expense in protecting the boy. I have to do what I think best."

"Only Simon?" Why would she put her brother's safety before her own? Certainly she realized Simon needed her.

"He seems to be her focus. I believe she's afraid they will come after him because he wasn't at the penthouse with their parents."

"Or could be they waited until they were certain he wasn't at home," Mitch offered.

"I told her that, too. Right now, she's too afraid to think rationally," Gary said. Mitch could hear a phone ringing in the background. "I'll get the ball rolling with the alarms. Have them overnighted. See if Tom can do the installation. I don't want to call attention to their presence by bringing in an alarm company. Gotta go."

Strange he'd mind someone seeing the alarms installed but

not the attention they'd bring to their location if they went off. Oh well, maybe the surrounding mountains would make it difficult to pinpoint where the sound was coming from. And the sirens would give them time to handle the situation before it got out of control.

A flash of green light caught his attention, jerking Mitch fully back to his patrol. His heart rate picked up. Someone was on the deck. He focused and saw Ari Kent sitting in the rocker. What was she doing out there this time of the night?

"It's Mitch," he called softly as he started to climb the stairs. Ari rose and came to stand by the rail.

"You're up late." Breathless from the steep climb, Mitch propped his arms on the rail next to her. He obviously needed to spend less time in his office chair and more time at the gym.

She typed into her phone and held it up for him to see.

"Can't sleep?" Mitch read aloud. "Is something bothering you? I've checked the area and there's no one out there."

Ari shrugged and pointed toward the house.

Mitch didn't want her to leave. "Don't go. Stay a few minutes. Just to talk."

Her phone acted like a night-light, and he caught her mocking look. "Okay, so I talk and you listen."

Ari returned to the rocker and sat down. Mitch settled in the chair next to hers.

She typed and turned her phone in his direction. *"Why are you working? I thought Tom had night shift."*

"Tom needs the rest."

More silence. This one-sided conversation took a great deal of work, Mitch decided. He looked out onto the valley. "This place is great. So peaceful."

From the first time his real estate agent brought him out to take a look, he'd been hooked by the privacy. He'd been looking for an investment and the two properties were perfect. A Realtor handled the leasing to tourists who wanted houses while visiting the mountains. And when life in Chicago got to be too much, he headed for the mountains and de-stressed.

But Ari didn't know these houses were his property. And Mitch knew Ari wouldn't like it if she knew the truth about him. He doubted a real-life psychiatrist would fit her idea of a security guard. "Gary ordered the alarms. Hopefully they won't scare you even worse if they go off."

She nodded and used her thumbs to type quickly into the phone. He marveled at her ability. His hunt-and-peck method took forever. Soon she held the phone for him to read.

"Whatever it takes. I'm afraid enough for both of us. I don't want Simon to suffer. But you're right about him being more aware. Neither of us gave any thought to the danger.

"Simon's not happy about being here," Ari typed. *"What do you remember about being seven?"*

"Not much," Mitch admitted. "Kids and the world have changed so much that my childhood experiences would be far different than Simon's."

"The only experiences I have with boys his age are those from school, and that's been more years than I care to count."

Mitch smiled and said, "Not that many."

"I'm 27."

He'd guessed right. "Simon's pretty young for all that's been dumped on him lately," Mitch agreed. "But he appears to be taking it all in stride."

"He doesn't understand why this happened any more than I do."

"But you're here for him, and that's the most important thing. I really would like to take him fishing," Mitch said, broaching the subject again.

She typed, *"Maybe later."*

"You're smart not to trust me yet," he said, hoping to

soothe her reservations about him. "I had the feeling earlier today that you would have come over that deck to take me out. You were aware of what was going on and focused on how to handle the situation Simon was in. That makes my job easier. I don't want him to be afraid, but he needs to keep his wits about him until the killer is found. My job is to keep you safe."

They sat in comfortable silence until he heard the soft sound of her breathing and realized she'd fallen asleep. Mitch opened the door and came back to gently lift Ari into his arms. He carried her inside and paused by the sofa. Deciding she'd be more comfortable in her bed, Mitch carried her into the master bedroom and laid her on the bed, pulling a blanket over her. He hoped she'd sleep away the remainder of the night as he removed the phone from her hand and turned it off, placing it on the nightstand.

four

"You're making my job too easy," Tom told Mitch over breakfast the next morning. "You took over all day yesterday, and now you want to take the family into Murphy today. Sure you won't fall asleep at the wheel?"

Mitch's first impression of the man had been of a dedicated soldier. Tom was older, his graying hair clipped in a neat military cut. He stood at medium height and was solidly built with a muscled chest and shoulders. A Texan, he wasn't the type to waste words and looked as if he could hold his own in a fight.

"I grabbed a couple of hours after you got up this morning," Mitch said. "I need to see how these outings work. Besides, the alarms should arrive today, and Gary said to ask if you'd do the install."

Tom nodded. "I told Gary Bishop he might as well take advantage of my experience. Former Navy Seal. Had a tough time when I left the service and Mr. Kent took a chance on me." He paused to butter another slice of toast. "I'm gonna find out what happened that night. Charles Kent was more than my boss. He was my friend."

Impressed by the man's loyalty, Mitch nodded. "Have you taken the three of them into Murphy before?"

"We stopped when we first arrived."

"I told Ari I didn't think it was a good idea."

Tom sighed. "Give it up. No matter how scared Ari might be, she won't allow Dora to go alone. That girl has a massive protector instinct when it comes to Simon and Dora."

"Dora?"

"The kids call her Nana, but her name is Dora Etheridge. She came to work for the Kents when Ari was born. Retired when Ari was sent off to boarding school, and then the Kents brought her back when Simon was born."

Mitch filed away the tidbit of information. His assessment of Dora Etheridge was the grandmotherly type. Her little more than five-foot frame was slightly stooped with her advanced years. Mitch suspected she was closer to seventy than sixty. She wore her salt-and-pepper hair in a tightly permed short cut and had a no-nonsense personality that he appreciated. She certainly didn't mind telling the Kents what she thought. "They wouldn't recognize the nanny."

"Not the same. Consider them a package deal. Where one goes, they all go."

"Do you think both of us should accompany them into Murphy?"

"It would call even more attention to them if we did. You'll find they're very cautious and look out for each other."

"What about other people? Do they pay attention?"

"Well," Tom said, his Texan drawl becoming more obvious, "Ari is a beautiful woman, and I've seen some admiring looks cast in her direction even when she tries to downplay her appearance."

Mitch didn't doubt that. Blond and beautiful made her most men's type. He certainly wasn't immune to her appearance. "How does she do that?"

"You'll see." Tom chuckled. "This trip could take a while. Dora likes to take time with her shopping. You may be going to more than one place. All purchases go on a Bishop credit card."

Mitch went to refill his coffee mug. He held up the pot and Tom shook his head.

He turned a wooden chair about and straddled it before taking a drink from his mug. "What's your gut telling you about the murders?"

Tom looked him straight in the eye and said, "Inside job. Place has private elevator access straight into the entrance and off the kitchen. Somebody had to let them into the penthouse."

Mitch caught the inference and wondered if Tom knew something the others didn't. "Them? You're thinking more than one?"

"Can't say for certain. The Kents could have been asleep or drugged."

"Gary said they had a party that night?"

Tom nodded. "A few close friends and business acquaintances. Their friends and that lawyer, Todd Langan, and his date, Ann Radnor. She worked for Mr. Kent in the past."

More names to file away. "Anyone else?" Mitch prompted.

"The other two couples were longtime acquaintances. Neither of them had anything to do with this."

"The lawyer?"

Tom frowned. "Hard to say. He's the pushy type. But Mr. K. shoved back when required. He would have me leave the window open when I drove them around so I could hear him give Langan fits over his legal advice."

"Why did Mr. Kent keep him around?"

"I asked him the same thing. He said Langan was a capable attorney, except for the times he was too pretentious for his own good."

Mitch considered that for a moment. "You think maybe Langan did something stupid?"

Tom shook his head. "Nah. Langan was out to impress the boss. Not kill him. Too bad Dora wasn't around that night."

"She might have been killed as well. I'm thinking the murderer planned things so everyone but the Kents would be out of the house."

Tom frowned. "That means they would have been aware of everyone's schedule."

"Possibly even someone they considered a friend. But what was their motive? Did they rob the Kents?"

"A few things were taken. Nothing worth killing anyone over."

Not much Mitch hadn't heard before. Did Langan resent the way Charles Kent had treated him? And he'd like to know more about this Ann woman. And who had the Kents trusted with their schedules? "Do you believe they intended to kill Ari and Simon as well?"

Tom crossed his arms and leaned back in the dining chair. "I plan to see to it that they don't get a chance."

Mitch nodded agreement. "I talked to Simon about being more aware yesterday." He described how he'd almost walked up on the child before Ari blew the whistle. "He was looking for a place to hide. That's why we're adding the alarms."

"Figured as much."

౫

Over at the other house, Ari drank coffee and ate a pastry as she read news on the Internet.

Behind her, withered hands opened and closed cabinet doors as Nana checked her grocery list, making noise as she pushed aside and rearranged items.

A can thudded on the hardwood floor, and Ari nearly jumped out of her chair.

"Sorry."

Ari retrieved the can and set it on the table. She was strung tighter than a fiddle with new strings. Was it because of the planned trip into Murphy? She wasn't about to let Nana go grocery shopping unassisted. The task would go quicker if she was there to help.

Nana brought her list over to the table. "Do you need any personal items?"

Ari shook her head.

"Better get dressed. Mitch will be here in a few minutes. I'll call Simon."

Mitch? How long did he think he could go without sleep?

When she'd awakened in her own bed that morning, Ari had been more than a little aware that she hadn't gotten there on her own. Why hadn't he left her in the rocker? She'd have made her way back to her room eventually.

As Nana predicted, Mitch arrived a few minutes later. Ari was dressed and Simon was downstairs changing into clean clothes.

She wrote on the whiteboard. *"Are you up to this? You didn't sleep last night."*

His smile was wide, his teeth strikingly white against his olive-toned skin.

"I'm good. Tom's an early riser so I managed a couple of hours' sleep before breakfast. He said Simon was down at the dock alone. Simon shouldn't be wandering about like that. We have to know where he is and what he's doing at all times. I'll talk to him."

❧

One look and Mitch understood what Tom meant by downplaying her looks. Ari wore very little makeup and her hair was braided down her back. Shades covered her eyes, and the capri pants and loose T-shirt didn't call attention to her body. Not many women her age could make themselves look younger, but Ari had managed to do exactly that.

The drive went pretty much as expected. The women opted to sit in the back of the SUV, leaving shotgun for Simon.

The boy rattled on for most of the trip. Mitch multitasked, driving, keeping up with the conversation, and paying close attention to what was going on around them. He wasn't used to children's chatter and was thankful when Nana suggested Simon give their ears a break. The child played games on his phone for the rest of the trip.

Mitch pulled into the parking lot at the tourism center.

"Anyone mind if we stop here?"

Simon looked up and asked curiously, "Where are we?"

Mitch killed the engine and opened his door. "Tourism center. Thought we might pick up some information on the area."

Nana chose to remain in the vehicle, but Ari and Simon joined him and plucked brochures from the covered board outside the building. Mitch found a couple of things that interested him.

"Anyone want to go inside for more information?" Mitch asked.

Both shook their heads, and they all returned to the vehicle. He drove on into town.

Mitch followed them into the store, taking note of their surroundings. He pushed the cart and told Simon to stay in front. The women walked together off to his right side. When a couple of guys focused their attention on Arianna, she moved closer to Mitch, taking his hand in hers. The men moved on and she let go, flashing him a smile as she did so.

Mitch noted that Ari walked faster in public, frequently glancing over her shoulder to see if anyone followed. He didn't doubt the not knowing who to trust gave her a feeling of overwhelming paranoia. For a couple of moments, he wondered why she'd put herself through this, but then he knew. Ari refused to give up completely. For Simon and Nana's sake, she would do everything she could to keep life as normal as possible. Even though there was absolutely nothing normal about their situation.

He saw Simon type into his phone and Arianna type something back. He appreciated that they used technology to communicate but thought how tiresome it must be not to be able to talk normally. When Simon and Nana spoke to each other, Mitch noted they didn't call each other by name. At times, Arianna e-mailed Simon, who in turn relayed the message to Nana. Too bad they didn't know sign language.

Simon lingered by an arrangement of rods and reels near the sports section of the store. "Are these the kind you use to fish?"

Mitch nodded. "I have several at the house. I'll loan you one and you can fish off the pier, if your sister is okay with that."

His questioning gaze turned in Arianna's direction.

She laughed, shaking her head at Mitch's determination to teach Simon how to fish. Ari texted her brother.

"Yes," came out like a hiss as he pumped his arm and his small face split wide with a grin.

She reached out and smoothed his wild hair.

"Ari says I can have one. Help me pick it out."

Mitch glanced at her and said, "There's plenty at the house."

She typed, *"Let him have his own. Maybe he'll become a great angler."*

They paused at the display while he removed a basic rod and reel he felt would work well for Simon. "We can buy bait at the marina."

"And then I'll catch one this big," Simon declared, throwing his arms open wide.

"Maybe." Mitch suspected the boy would be surprised by the size of his first fish. "I think you can fish on my license. I'll check to be sure. You know, there's more to this than fishing. You have to learn the angler's creed. And always eat what you catch."

"Speaking of eating, let's get this shopping done," Nana said.

The group followed the older woman up and down the aisles, retrieving the items she called out from her list. Soon the groceries were paid for and loaded in the back of the SUV. Simon's new fishing pole had been relegated to the back when Nana said he'd poke out someone's eye if he kept it in front with him.

Mitch liked the older woman's practical mind-set. She said what she felt and the Kents respected her. Back at the house, he helped carry the groceries inside. Arianna sent Nana off to rest while she unpacked the bags and put the items away. Simon took his new rod and reel down to his playroom. Mitch cautioned him not to remove it from the package until they could assemble it together.

"Did you rest okay last night?" Mitch asked, shifting some of the canned goods into the pantry cabinet.

Ari blushed and nodded.

Mitch halted next to her. "You're embarrassed that I carried you to bed?"

She nodded.

"I couldn't leave you out there in the night air, and I thought you'd be more comfortable in your bed than on the sofa." Mitch emptied and folded the last bag. "Nothing to feel ashamed about. I'd better find Tom and see if those alarms arrived."

Ari mouthed, *Thank you.*

&

After finishing in the kitchen, Arianna took her Bible out to the deck. One of her resolutions had been to read through the Bible in a year again, and despite all that had happened, she'd managed to stay on target with her reading. God had granted her a great deal of peace and knowledge in these daily sessions.

She missed her church. It had been a key part of her life ever since she gave her life to Christ. And now when she felt she needed it most, she couldn't attend.

Dear Lord, she prayed silently, *please be with me as I struggle to overcome this fear and regain my voice. Guide the police in their search for my parents' murderers and give us strength to deal with the outcome. Shield us from harm.*

And bless me in the reading of Your Word and give me a clear understanding of what I read.

Ari's biggest regret was not being able to share her love for the Lord with her parents. They didn't tell her she was crazy for making the decision, but they weren't interested in hearing about what had changed her. She'd witnessed to them at every opportunity but hadn't touched their hearts with her message.

When she'd gone off to boarding school, Ari doubted her parents suffered from empty nest syndrome. She hadn't wanted to go, but they felt the experience would polish her and prepare her for college. Though she'd missed her parents and Nana, she had survived.

Her first year of college was all-consuming, and Ari relished each new experience. She lived in one of the dorms, made her own decisions, chose her own friends, and dated when she wanted.

Her roommate was a believer and invited Ari to attend church with her. Shannon never gave up, repeating the invitation every time she left for church until the night Ari said yes.

By Christmas of her sophomore year, Ari had accepted Christ as her Savior. His love was more than sufficient and she'd stopped thinking about the must-do activities of college and focused on her must-do list for Christian life.

Ari came home for winter break to find her parents traveling overseas. She could have joined them but chose to spend the holidays in Chicago. As usual, the house was beautifully decorated and there were gifts under the tree. Ari had thought maybe they planned to have a party for the New Year.

When Ari called to ask if Nana had time for a visit, she encouraged her former charge to come immediately. Ari stayed with Nana through Christmas. Nana was pleased to hear that Ari had given her life to Christ. Her parents had not returned by the time she returned to school after the New Year.

By spring break, Simon was nearly a month old and Dora Etheridge was living with the Kent family. Ari hugged Nana and asked, "Why didn't you tell me you were coming back?"

"Didn't know myself until a few days ago."

She handed Simon over and Ari cuddled her tiny baby brother close to her chest. She went in search of her mother. "Why didn't you tell me?"

Michelle Kent wore a designer suit and expensive shoes, not a hair out of place and her makeup flawless as she thumbed through a fashion magazine. She looked nothing like a woman who had recently become a mother at the age of forty-four. "We missed you at Christmas."

"But we talked and you never said a word."

"We weren't sure about the outcome."

Concerned that her mother's pregnancy had been risky, Ari said, "You should have told me. I could have come home."

Tiny lines creased her mother's forehead. "You have your own life now, Arianna."

Her arms tightened protectively around the tiny bundle swathed in a soft knitted blue shawl that Ari knew had to be Nana's work. She nuzzled his cheek, loving the sweet baby smell of him. "He has Daddy's hair and eyes."

"Ari, do take him back to Nana," her mother exclaimed suddenly. "You'll throw him off schedule."

"But Mom. . ."

"Take the baby back to Nana," she repeated sternly. "I don't want him upset. He already cries enough as it is."

Ari looked up and demanded, "Why does he cry?"

"The pediatrician said his formula didn't agree with him. You never had problems like that."

"Poor baby," Ari cooed. "Did that nasty old formula make you sick?"

"It's been changed and he's doing better. Take him back to Nana."

Reluctantly she returned Simon to the perfectly decorated nursery. She kissed his cheek one last time and started to place him in the wooden cradle.

Nana sat in a rocker next to a fireplace that burned merrily as her fingers moved the knitting needles in perfect precision. "Babies need love."

"But Mom says I'll disrupt his schedule," she repeated, feeling confused by her nanny's contradictory message.

Nana indicated the bottle in the warmer and the second rocker. She continued to knit as Ari fed Simon for the first time. After a while, she followed Nana's instructions and burped him. Eventually he slept. Ari snuggled him closer and set the bottle on the table. She was in love with this little guy. She looked at her long-ago caregiver. "Did Mom have a difficult time with the birth?"

Nana shrugged. "Couldn't say. They called me after Simon was born."

Twenty years before, Michelle Kent had lured the older, well-established nanny away from another family when Ari was born. After ten years of caring for her sole charge, Nana retired at the age of fifty-two. She'd gone to live outside Chicago near her family. Ari remained in touch with the woman she loved like a grandmother. Nana was sixty-two when the Kents called her back into service.

"I told your mother I'm too old, but she pleaded with me to come back. Said they would hire extra help if I needed someone."

Ari looked down at the bundle in her arms. "I can't believe they didn't tell me." Had her mother been so overwhelmed by the news that she hadn't known what to say? They should consider themselves blessed. Sure, her mom was older, but she was in good physical condition. And she had given Charles Kent the son he'd always wanted.

Ari knew that about her father. More than anything in life, he'd wanted a son. She knew he must be thrilled beyond words. In a way, her inability to measure up hurt, and yet she found it difficult to harbor a grudge against her baby brother.

Yet strangely enough Charles Kent seemed equally distant from Simon. Ari knew her parents weren't typical parental examples. Simon's childhood experience was similar to her own. Their parents had left it to Nana to provide their children with unending love.

Simon's arrival changed her world. Ari returned to college but looked forward to the times she could be home with Simon and Nana. She loved him and there was nothing she wouldn't do for him. That included keeping him safe now.

After graduation, at a time in her life when she could have gone anywhere and tried anything, Ari knew she had to come home. Her parents left the majority of Simon's care to Nana, and Ari wanted to take some of the stress of caring for the active little boy off the woman.

Her off-work hours were dedicated to church and her brother. Thankfully her parents hadn't objected to her taking Simon to church, and Ari was glad the child enjoyed himself enough to want to go back. Now she could only hope their parents had listened when she spoke to them of Jesus.

The click of the door opening snapped her back to the present. Mitch stepped outside.

"Just wanted to let you know the alarms are connected. No more worries that anyone will slip up on you and Simon. Tom says they'll make a lot of noise, so be prepared."

Better to frighten people than for us to die, Ari thought.

"The fingerprint door lock on the lower floor is in place as well. We'll need to get everyone registered." He pointed to her cell. "I noticed you use your phone to communicate," Mitch said. "Would you like to learn sign language? I'd be happy to show you the alphabet and a few phrases that might help simplify your communication."

Ari shook her head negatively. To her, learning sign language showed acceptance of the situation. She would never accept that her voice wouldn't return.

"Let me know if you change your mind. Oh, here's the mail we picked up."

All mail was forwarded to a post office box for Bishop Security, which in turn had it delivered to a post office box in Murphy for pickup.

Ari thanked Mitch and watched as he disappeared from sight before she flipped through the correspondence looking for anything of importance. Most items had already been forwarded via e-mail. There were sympathy and memorial donation cards from friends and acquaintances and one envelope from the attorney.

A frown creased her forehead as she slit open the envelope from Todd Langan. She read through the papers, breathing a relieved sigh when she found they were copies of a follow-up report on another hotel the chain was considering.

No doubt Todd Langan wasn't happy that he had to communicate with her through the security company. She knew the brief handwritten note instructing her to contact him as soon as possible for the reading of the will had been his reason for this snail mail.

Since Todd hadn't been involved in the writing of her parents' will, Ari wasn't sure why he thought he would have anything to do with the probate.

While she knew it had to be done, Ari needed time. Her parents were barely in their graves. Day-to-day operation of the business had not stopped. Her father had always kept competent people in place to assure the business continued as usual in his absence, and Ari knew it wouldn't stop in hers either.

Her knitting lay in the basket at her feet, and she reached for the soft baby blanket. It was a gift for her sales manager, who expected her first child around Christmas. Most days her frustrations eased as she worked the yellow yarn into the design. The soothing quality of the activity took over and occupied her hands if not her mind.

But not today. She couldn't concentrate. This wasn't what she needed to be doing. She should be in Chicago, running her hotel and doing the things she enjoyed in life. She should be visiting her parents and sharing God's love for them. Not hiding in the mountains grieving their loss. Frustrated, Ari stabbed the needles into the ball of yarn and shoved it back into the basket.

Maybe she should see the specialists as Dr. Graves suggested. No. She had to help herself. She needed to try harder.

Ari considered her changed attitude since the loss of her parents and her voice. Always a strong-willed woman, she now felt defenseless, the fight drained from her. Nothing else mattered but keeping Simon safe. Seeking escape from her thoughts, she rose from the chair and went in search of her brother.

She found the child in one of the lower-floor bathrooms—his laboratory, as he called the room. Simon often bolted here when he tired of female companionship. He messed around with weird concoctions for hours, his intelligent young mind eagerly absorbing every drop of knowledge. He routinely requested more equipment and books when he mastered what he already had.

At his age, she'd barely been reading, but he was reading a couple of grades above his age level. She handed over the games that Shannon had sent, and he laid them on the countertop.

"Hey Ari, watch this," he said, adding a mint to a diet soda bottle. The soda shot up like a geyser from the bottle. "Cool, huh?"

She nodded. Luckily for him, he'd thought to place his experiment in the shower stall. Ari gestured upstairs and made the motion of eating.

"A few more minutes," he begged, his green gaze pleading in a manner that melted the best of intentions. Maybe she should allow Mitch to take the boy fishing. He needed companionship.

Ari relented, holding up ten fingers. She gestured upstairs with her thumb, making it clear that she expected him to be washed up and at the table in exactly that amount of time.

❧

After dinner at the other house, Tom said, "Think I'll catch a nap before my shift."

Mitch nodded. "I'll do a walk-around." He turned off the dock and perimeter alarms, leaving the driveway alarm activated during his prowl.

His thoughts turned to what Ari was doing. They were out on the deck, playing something on a boom box. What was it? Mitch paused, listening as different voices read aloud. He walked a few steps farther and sat down on the bottom step.

"I like this," Simon said, his childish voice eager and enthusiastic.

Mitch wished Ari could respond. He wanted nothing more than to hear her speak. He fantasized about her voice, imagining it to be soft and sweet.

More than anything he wanted an opportunity to get to know her better and share the truth about himself with her. She was a special woman. Would she be willing to think of him as more than a security guard?

He was a doctor with good standing in the medical community. More than suitable for her. But then, he didn't feel Ari worried about things like that.

The changing voices in the work being read caught his attention and Mitch agreed with Simon. It was interesting—the reading as dramatic as any theater.

The Bible, Mitch realized. Actors read from the book of Exodus when Moses led the children of Israel from Egypt. Sound effects, including horses whinnying, chariots moving, and the sea receding, gave even more realism to the reading.

"Sweet," Simon exclaimed at the conclusion. "Can we listen to more?"

Mitch could imagine Ari's smile of pleasure. He heard footsteps on the deck and shot up from the steps, not wanting to get caught eavesdropping. Simon came to the railing.

"Mitch, hey," he said, waving at him. "Come on up."

He made his way up the stairs with a rapidness that astonished him. Eagerness to see Ari? He'd noticed how often she was in his thoughts. No other woman had ever managed to occupy his mind like that.

He and Simon knuckle bumped and he smiled at Ari. An easy smile played at the corners of her mouth. Their eyes met and held for several seconds before she broke away.

"What are you two up to on this fine evening?"

"Listening to an audio Bible. It's cool. You should come and listen, too," Simon invited. "We went to Bible study at home. Ari likes to discuss the Bible. She teaches the three-year-olds' class at church."

Mitch looked at her. She shrugged.

"I bet you're good with them." An overwhelming sadness filled her expression. "Miss them?"

She nodded.

"She likes doing fun things with them. Sometimes I help, don't I, Ari?" His sister nodded. "She says I'm a big help. I like it, too. At least they don't cry a lot like the real little babies."

"Hey champ, that's their way of communicating. Did you

know that parents can tell whether they're sick or hungry or need a diaper change by the way they cry?"

"No kidding?"

Mitch could see the suggestion intrigued the boy. "No kidding. Guess I'd better get back out there and finish my walk-around. Tom's on tonight," he said to Ari, wondering if she would miss their midnight chat as much as he would.

Simon bounded to his feet. "Can I come with you?"

Mitch glanced at Ari. "I've already checked most of the area, so it'll be a stroll down to the dock and back up the hill."

She nodded and the two of them left as she picked up the box of CDs and went inside.

five

The next morning dawned dismally gray. The mountains hid behind a layer of fog and storm clouds, giving the area an entirely different atmosphere. Ari supposed it was one of the reasons they were called the Smoky Mountains. She glanced at the clock and realized the outer dimness made her room dark. She crawled from the bed, still tired after only four hours' sleep. No Mitch to keep her company last night. She'd heard Tom making his rounds, but he hadn't come up the stairs to find her on the deck.

China rattled in the kitchen. Nana was already up and at work. Ari fought back her natural concern for the elderly woman.

Ari insisted they could cope for themselves so that she could get more rest, but Nana pshawed the idea, reassuring her she wasn't old enough to take life that easy. Ari disagreed. Sixty-nine was plenty old enough. Maybe she should check into hiring someone to prepare meals while they were here.

She dragged herself to the bathroom. Quickly braiding her long hair, she tucked it underneath the shower cap and stepped beneath the spray. The cold water did the trick. Ari felt wide-awake as she stepped out and toweled herself. Slipping on a short white toweling robe, she went to her room and dressed in jean shorts and a cool cotton top. She moved around the bedroom, making the bed and putting her clothes in the hamper, chores she knew Nana would do if she didn't.

"Morning, Ari," Nana called with a smile, setting a plate of bacon and eggs on the table. "You're later than usual this morning."

Ari glanced at her watch. A few minutes after eight. Late? Only Nana would think that. Bowing her head, she said a silent prayer before picking up the fork. Thunder rumbled as she took her first bite.

She pulled a whiteboard over to her and wrote, *"Where is Simon?"*

"Last I saw of him, he had that fishing pole and was headed for the dock. He needs to come inside."

Simon needed to stop disappearing like this. Had Mitch talked to him yet? Exasperated that he had gone outside with a storm brewing, Ari wiped her mouth and dropped the napkin on the table. The boy might be smart, but he wouldn't come in because of something as trivial as a thunderstorm. Ari slid her feet into a pair of sneakers.

Once outside, she quickened her step, hoping to find Simon and get back inside before it got any worse. Jagged streaks of lightning lit the dark sky. Thunder rolled ominously and the winds gusted.

From the deck, she looked down at the dock and panicked when she didn't see him anywhere. Had Simon gone in on the lower floor? Then she spotted the rod and reel lying at the base of the stairs. Something had happened. Ari knew how fastidious Simon was with his things. He'd never leave the new fishing gear lying around like that.

She raced down the steep stairs, frantically surveying the surrounding area. The lot around the house had been cleared except for the low undergrowth along the hillside. The forest picked up where the lot ended.

At the bottom, Ari raced back and forth across the cleared area near the water. No sign of Simon. Ari jumped onto the dock to get a better view. The deafening wail of the alarm started about the same time as the torrential downpour that soaked her hair and clothing in seconds. She shivered, closing her eyes when a lightning strike seemed too close for comfort. She'd hated storms since the age of six when she'd gotten lost in the park.

Where were Mitch and Tom? Why weren't they here? Terrified, she started up the pathway, her shoes filling with the water that channeled down the hill. Where was Simon? Had he been kidnapped? Taken by an intruder? Ari began to shake as the fearful images filled her thoughts.

࿏

At the first sound of the alarm, Mitch shot out of the other house, jerking on his raincoat as he ran. He saw Ari working her way up the hill, soaking wet and obviously frightened. What had happened? He ran to where she stood and clutched her shoulders. "What's wrong?" He shouted to be heard over the storm and the sirens.

Her blue eyes glittered with fear, stark and vivid, as she gestured toward the dock. *Simon,* she mouthed frantically. Her hand measured a distance from the ground.

Another lightning strike. Mitch grabbed Ari's hand and tugged, yelling again, "Come on. Let's get out of the storm."

She gasped, all but panting in terror as she struggled against him. She mouthed Simon's name again.

"Simon?" He looked around. "Where is he?"

She raised her hands, palms out, shaking her head in desperation. Ari struggled to break free to continue her search. She started to run off, slipped in the mud, and fell.

Mitch lifted her to her feet and looked her in the eyes. "Ari, go inside. I'll call Tom." She struggled against him, tears intermingling with raindrops. "Stop fighting me," he ordered, tightening his hold. "Look at me." She lifted her gaze to his. "We'll find Simon. No one has been in the area. You set the alarm off when you came down to the dock. Now go upstairs before you get hurt. I'll find him."

Worry was plain on her face as she took a step toward the house. "Go," he repeated.

Mitch kept glancing her way to make sure she was moving as he viewed the area. He ran and slid down the hill, toward the dock, thankful when Tom killed the piercing sirens. He could barely think with all that noise ringing in his ears.

Rain poured from the black skies as thunder boomed and brilliant flashes of lightning helped to light his way. He saw Ari's tiny footprints in the mud. She'd already checked these areas. He began to trek back and forth across the lot, pulling back the low vegetation that could hide a small boy.

He glanced up and saw Ari and Nana standing on the deck. The agony on their faces nearly did him in. Mitch neared the edge of the wooded area and heard something strange. Almost like something or someone crying.

"Simon?" he yelled. "Is that you, buddy? Talk to me. Where are you?"

"Mitch."

The weak cry was music to his ears. He cupped his hands around his mouth and yelled up to them. "He's here." He watched as Ari turned into Nana's open arms and allowed the woman to comfort her.

"Mitch?"

"I'm here, buddy." He jerked the ground cover out of the way and spotted Simon crumpled in a rocky depression.

Blood flowed from a gash on Simon's forehead. Mitch quickly assessed the situation. The cut would require a couple of stitches.

"What happened?"

Simon groaned, his face wet with rain and tears. "Tripped on a rock. Hit my head. Hurts," he whispered.

"Does anything else hurt?"

"My leg."

A quick examination told him Simon had broken his right fibula. Mitch debated taking time to find a brace but decided they needed to get out of this storm. "I'm going to carry you back to the house."

"I can. . ."

Simon trailed off, his face blanching white when Mitch lifted him from the ground. He watched the boy's face, seeing the tears that trailed along his cheeks. "Hang on, buddy. I'll have you there in a minute."

Mitch entered the house through the lower door. He cradled Simon against his body and leaned to place his finger on the lock and hit the handle. "We're downstairs," he bellowed once they were inside.

Carrying Simon into the nearest bedroom, Mitch settled him on the bed, jerking the covers over his small wet body. Ari and Tom ran into the room.

"Get me some towels," Mitch demanded.

Tom ran into the bathroom and returned with a big stack of clean towels. Mitch wrapped one around Simon's shoulders and used another to dry his hair. Another stemmed the flow of blood from his forehead.

"We need dry clothes," he said. "Better make it loose shorts. His leg is broken."

He saw Ari take a deep breath and go white. She had seen the blood. He pushed her down onto the end of the bed.

"Put your head between your knees," Mitch directed, his firm hands pushing her head forward. She hung suspended for several minutes. "Better?" he asked when she tried to sit up.

She nodded.

"Good. He needs to have that leg set. What's your doctor's name?" Mitch didn't let on that he already knew the Kents' doctor. "We'll call and see if he knows of an orthopedic in the area willing to set Simon's leg in his office."

"I'll do it," Tom said as he handed over the dry clothing. "You need to change, too."

"Later." He used one of the towels to swipe at his hair and face. Mitch caught Ari's uncertain expression and suggested,

"Why don't you help Nana make cocoa? Hot and sweet. It will help warm him up." After she'd gone, Mitch looked at Tom and said, "We need something to splint his leg."

"There were some lengths of heavy cardboard on the packaging for the alarms. I stuck it down in the basement for recycling. We can use that and some duct tape," Tom said. "Bone come through?"

Mitch shook his head. "Clean break. We can put it back in place."

Tom grimaced and glanced down at Simon. The boy lay with his eyes closed. "Think he can handle it?"

"Probably better than trying to get him to the doctor like it is."

"I'll get the material and make that call. And get you a dry shirt."

Mitch toweled Simon and dressed him in dry clothes. He pulled the comforter over the wet place on the bed and covered Simon with a dry blanket. He held the cup of cocoa Ari handed him as Simon sipped and blew. "Still cold?"

"I'm good."

Mitch admired Simon's effort to put on a good front as the boy shivered against his chest. Mitch hitched the blanket up around his shoulders. "What were you doing out there?"

"Nothing."

Mitch knew from the slightly defensive edge in his voice that Simon was lying. "I saw the fishing pole," he said. "It's out there in the rain."

Simon looked guilty. "You've been busy. I thought maybe you'd have time to help me today."

Mitch smiled. He'd once been an impatient boy himself. He'd become pretty anxious a few times when an adult promised him something and seemed in no hurry to carry through.

He rubbed the towel over Simon's head again. "It's okay. They're made to withstand water."

Tom returned with the supplies.

"Simon, this is going to hurt, but it'll be easier for you if we set the leg now. Think you can handle it?"

The boy nodded. Mitch looked at Ari. "What about you?" She nodded. "Sit here next to him and hold his hand."

Simon's skin turned whiter as he fought the pain of setting the bone, but he only cried out once.

"Good job," Mitch comforted with a pat on the arm. "We're going to splint your leg and then we'll take you to the doctor."

After it was over and Simon lay back, Mitch said, "I need to change my shirt. Don't let him move too much."

Mitch pulled his golf shirt over his head as he walked into the big room and used the towel around his neck to dry his hair.

He heard a gasp and turned around to see Ari standing behind him. She covered her mouth with her hand.

She'd seen the scars. "I nearly died in a fire when I was thirteen."

Ari's eyes drifted closed. Mitch took a step forward, preparing to catch her if she fell. She touched her forehead.

Thankful she'd chosen not to dwell on his own injuries, Mitch said, "He banged his head when he fell. Head wounds bleed a lot."

She mouthed, *Thank you*, and went back to Simon.

Mitch went upstairs and took the cup Nana handed him. He walked over to the glass wall. The storm had blown over. Rain pattered lightly on the deck, an occasional distant streak of lightning flashing in the sky. Thunder rumbled far off.

The idea that Ari's fear might have triggered the return of her voice niggled at him. Why hadn't the words come when she tried to tell him Simon was missing? What would it take to bring back her voice?

Mitch considered how bad the storm had been. Ari never

should have gone off like that. Why hadn't she blown her whistle? Done something to alert them? They wouldn't have known she was out there in the storm if she hadn't set off the alarm. She could have hurt herself badly while running around on that hill. He needed her to understand that the purpose of having security was to depend on them to take care of things. Time to lay out a few ground rules for both of them.

❧

"Hi, Ari," Simon said sleepily.

She smiled and touched his cheek. Ari longed to throw her arms around his small frame but contented herself with sitting on the edge of the bed next to him.

"I messed up, didn't I?"

Ari nodded and wished she could tell him no harm done. Instead he would have to deal with the inconvenience this break was going to cause. For weeks to come his world would become even more limited.

"Mitch and Tom did a neat job on my leg," he said, flinging back the covers to show her. "Tom got this cardboard from a package. It's really hard and folded in a V. They taped it like a box." He tapped the cardboard with his fist.

Tom came into the room, waving a piece of paper, Mitch right behind him. "Dr. Graves says this guy is willing to set Simon's leg and keep quiet. He has X-ray equipment in his office and will do it after hours. We're supposed to be there at six."

"Can Simon wait that long?" Nana asked as she stepped into the room.

Mitch smiled reassuringly at her. "We've done what we can to make him comfortable. He's tough. Barely cried out when we set his leg."

Nana frowned. "How did you do that?"

"I've seen it done," Mitch said, hoping she would accept his answer.

"I'm going with you," Ari jotted onto a piece of paper on the nightstand.

"You'll have to. You're Simon's guardian." He glanced at Tom. "Let's get blankets and pillows and make a bed in the SUV for Simon."

"Stay with them," Tom said. "I'll handle it."

Ari touched the white gauze taped to Simon's forehead.

"How are you feeling, buddy? Dizzy? Light-headed?"

Ari was thankful when Mitch asked the questions she needed answered.

"Okay."

"Ready to get that leg casted?"

Simon looked apprehensive.

Mitch's hand came to rest on Simon's shoulder. "The worst is over. You'll soon be up and about on your crutches. I broke my leg when I was about your age and it healed as good as new."

"I scared Ari."

Mitch nodded. "Yeah, she thought you were out there playing Ben Franklin in that storm. Told her you didn't have a kite," he teased. "Didn't anyone tell you not to stand under trees when it's lightning?"

"I couldn't get up. My head and leg hurt real bad. I was cold and wet. I yelled, but the storm was too loud."

He patted Simon's shoulder. "I know, buddy."

Ari sat there, a silent onlooker as Mitch reassured the child. He was good with Simon. Mitch always seemed to know the right thing to say. Ari noted a little color had come back to Simon's cheeks.

"He's all boy," Mitch said to Ari. "I can't tell you how many broken bones I had."

Simon never had any until she brought him here to keep him safe, Ari thought. She knew better than to blame herself. It could have happened to anyone. Didn't the child have enough problems? He'd be miserable being stuck inside.

"I'm sorry, Ari," he said sleepily.

She wrote him a note. *"I'm OK if you're OK."*

"I'm good," he said. "I went down that hill like a rubber ball. Except I don't bounce."

His giggle brought a smile to her face. Everything would be fine.

six

The doctor hadn't asked questions beyond those related to Simon's injuries. He x-rayed the leg and casted it in the denim-colored fiberglass Simon chose when Mitch suggested he might want to choose something a little less obvious than fluorescent orange. He even stitched up the cut on the boy's forehead and gave them the go-ahead to take him home. Mitch paid for his services with a Bishop credit card.

Back at the house, they ate a late supper and Ari suggested Simon take her room or sleep in the second bed in Nana's room.

"No. I want to sleep in my room," Simon said, sounding tired and whiny.

"Ari and Nana have to monitor you overnight," Mitch said.

Simon didn't say anything.

Ari looked at Mitch from her place behind the sofa and shook her head.

"Okay buddy, sunroom it is."

Simon nodded.

Earlier the boy had insisted he could make it into the house on his own with the new crutches. The steps had proven to be too much for him. After Simon was settled comfortably on the sofa bed with his favorite book, Mitch said good night and left.

❧

Around ten, while doing his perimeter search, Mitch called Dwayne Graves. "Sorry it's so late, but I thought you'd like an update. It was a clean break. The doctor handled the situation himself."

"Know him from medical school. He's a good guy. How's Ari?"

"She calmed down once the doctor told her Simon would probably be back to normal within a month."

"I wondered if she spoke."

Mitch had his own thoughts on the matter. Given her reaction, he was almost surprised that she hadn't expressed herself verbally. "There was a time there when I thought I'd have two patients. She nearly passed out when she saw the blood from the head wound. Probably experienced a flashback of her parents' bedroom."

"Poor kids. Have you told her yet?"

"No," Mitch said. "I'm working security, Dwayne."

"Why would it matter?"

"You know why. Once the truth comes out, everything changes. Let me do my bit to keep them safe. I'm qualified."

"Okay, Mitch. I trust you to do what's right."

What was right? He might have started this out of some sort of sympathy, but facing an unknown enemy together made them friends. Would Ari be upset when she learned the truth about his real profession?

"Thanks for letting me know about Ari and Simon. Take care of them."

"I'm trying. They're pretty determined."

Dwayne chuckled. "Man, you're preaching to the choir. Thanks for calling."

Mitch turned off the phone and tucked it into his pocket. Ari's reaction to Simon's injury had been pretty strong. Had the shock made things worse rather than better? Had fear pushed her ability to speak even further away? Maybe he should find a specialist—someone experienced with conversion disorder who could tell him what to expect.

Their fear really bothered him. As far as he was concerned, Ari and Simon had received a raw deal. Neither of them deserved this horror that pervaded their lives. And he would do everything possible to make sure they weren't hurt again.

Mitch found Arianna Kent intriguing. Over the years, he'd met a number of spoiled wealthy women, some socially and others in the course of his work. Ari was nothing like them. Despite her fears, she exuded a peace he found fascinating. Was it her focus on God that carried her through the tough times? He sure would like to know. Maybe he should ask.

Mitch let himself into the house and found Ari dozing on the sofa. He'd noticed she wasn't on the deck when he checked the area earlier. He should have known she'd remain close to Simon.

He went into the sunroom and gently shook Simon awake. "How's your head, buddy?"

"Hurts."

Mitch went through the questions, waiting for Simon's groggy replies. "You want something for your head?"

"I'm okay."

He patted his shoulder and said, "Go back to sleep. I'll check on you again later."

He adjusted the pile of pillows underneath Simon's leg and made sure his covers were in place before going back into the other room.

He bumped against a stack of books and they fell over. Ari jumped to her feet.

"Sorry." He bent down to pick them up.

She sat down on the sofa, reaching for her whiteboard. *"Is he okay?"*

"He's got a bit of a headache, but that's to be expected. I took him through the doctor's checklist and he passed with flying colors."

She relaxed a little. *"Figures I'd fall asleep the night I need to be alert."*

He'd gotten into the habit of joining her for a midnight

rendezvous each night he was on duty. They talked until Ari decided she could sleep.

"Why don't you go to bed? I'll check in with him every hour or so."

"I'll stay in case he needs me."

"He's already asleep."

"I feel so inadequate," she wrote on the board.

Tears started to trickle along her cheeks.

Mitch sat down next to her. "Come here," he whispered, pulling her into his arms. "You're not, Ari," he crooned as he held her close. "Simon's lucky to have you."

Her arms tightened around him as they sat there silently. Neither attempted to break free. The tears flowed and she trembled in his hold. Had she allowed herself to cry like this since her parents' death? Like most men, Mitch wasn't comfortable with tears, but he knew their healing power.

After a while, she started to sniff. He pulled tissues from the box on the table and placed them in her hand.

They separated. She dabbed at her face and reached for the board. *"He's hurt, Mitch. I should have done a better job of protecting him."*

His brown gaze met hers as he said, "He's a boy, Ari. You can't watch him every minute. You're lucky he hasn't broken something long before now."

He'd taken more than a few forays into dangerous territories and knew the risks Simon faced as a curious child.

"Don't beat yourself up about this. It's not your fault. None of what's happened to you is your fault."

"It's going to make the situation even harder for him and everyone else."

"We'll manage. In a day or so, Simon will be on the mend doing all the things he did before. You'll see. That cast won't hold him back."

She managed a tiny smile and scribbled, *"Thanks for letting me cry on your shoulder."*

He took her hand. "It's yours anytime you need. I know you're trying to be strong for Simon, but it is okay to show your emotions. You've suffered a grievous loss that has affected you in a big way. You have a right to feel afraid. Have you considered keeping a journal? It would be a good way to get those feelings out that you can't share normally. Do it for yourself."

"God already hears most of my concerns," she wrote. *"The mental dialogue with Him helps."*

"I've been meaning to ask you about that. Is the peace you exude a result of your relationship with God?"

Ari brushed an errant curl out of her face. *"I don't feel I'm exuding peace."*

"Probably because of the fear. Maybe I feel at peace when I'm around you."

"I'd like to believe that people see God in my every action," she wrote. *"At times like this when I know how strong God is, I feel extremely weak."*

"You don't always have to be in control, Ari. I promise no one will consider you a total wreck if you shed a few tears or show your fears. Those who know the truth will share those emotions."

"Thanks, Mitch. How do you always know what to say?"

He didn't tell her that years of education and professional experience guided his efforts to advise others, and he hoped he said the right things to give them comfort.

Instead he squeezed her hand. "It's been so crazy around here today that I forgot to tell you Gary called this morning. He plans to come Sunday afternoon. He wants to bring Jennifer and Will with him."

"Why is he coming?"

"Said he wants to see things for himself and determine if any improvements can be made. Did I tell you Jennifer is my sister?"

Ari shook her head.

"Jen and Gary met back when I first worked for Bishop."

She looked puzzled.

"I've recently started working for them again," Mitch explained, not adding that it was a volunteer job.

Ari wrote, *"Nana would like to celebrate her birthday in Asheville with her sister. She wants to leave on Sunday if you don't think it's a problem. I'd like either you or Tom to escort her."*

"I'll talk to Tom. I'd like to stick around here, but if he doesn't agree, I'll go. We can celebrate her birthday Saturday night. Maybe grill out so she doesn't have any reason to be in the kitchen."

"I ordered a cake."

"Sounds good." He needed to get back to work. "How are the nerves?"

She shrugged.

"This is why Simon needs to check in with us before he goes wandering. It could have been more of a life-and-death situation if that head injury had been worse."

"I hate restricting him even more," Ari wrote.

"As his guardian, you'll have to establish rules. I'm sure your parents did."

Her skin paled.

"I'm sorry," Mitch said.

"My parents didn't supervise Simon. That's Nana's job. She coordinates his schedule. Tom drives him around."

"Did your parents spend time with Simon?"

"Not as much as he would have liked. Daddy was at the office and Mom had her social activities. They did try to have family dinners with us on Sunday nights."

At least Simon had that much, though Mitch doubted their Sunday night experiences were like the dinners he'd had with his family. They were required to be at the table at seven sharp every night. No excuses. They were expected to do their homework before dinner. Once at the table, they discussed their days and then after dinner sometimes watched television together or had movie nights or played games.

He appreciated the sacrifice his parents made for him and Jen. No doubt they were exhausted after their long days. His dad had been a pharmacist and his mom a nurse in a doctor's office.

"I tried to take some of the load off Nana whenever possible. Simon entertains himself a lot. After I came home I made a point of coming over a couple of nights each week to eat dinner with him. Afterward we snuggled and watched movies or I read to him." She stopped writing and smiled. *"He used to read with me. I thought he was a genius. I didn't realize he'd memorized his favorite books. I tucked him in and said his bedtime prayers with him. He was such a sweet little guy. Still is, but he's changing."*

"Growing up on you?"

She nodded. *"I know it's going to happen, but it scares me. I don't know anything about boys."*

"Nothing?" Mitch teased.

She fiddled with the marker cap, popping it on and off the pen. *"Dating isn't the same as raising a male child."*

"Don't most women think of men as overgrown little boys?" he asked with a grin.

"Some guys act that way."

Mitch couldn't deny that even he acted like a child at times. "You could get your dates involved in activities with Simon."

"Doesn't work. Most aren't looking for a big sister / little brother combo to date. They want to lose the kid or pawn him off on someone else."

Mitch hadn't considered that. "What do you do?"

"Lose the guy as quickly as possible. Simon's important to me and I'm looking for a take me, take my brother kind of man."

Mitch didn't find that unrealistic. When he found the right woman, he hoped to be as close to her family as he was to Jen. "You'll find the man who accepts Simon as part of your life and doesn't think of him as a straggler. Want some advice?"

Her expression indicated she did.

"Take everything one day at a time. And remember change is necessary for him to become a well-adjusted adult. Whether he slides through puberty without angst or he struggles along the way, remind yourself that it will pass."

"Thanks, Mitch, but days like today make it difficult to believe I can handle the responsibility."

"Oh, I suspect you'll come through with flying colors, Arianna Kent. You strike me as the kind of woman who could mother a dozen children without losing control."

She seemed surprised by his comment. *"Maybe if I never get my voice back. I imagine kids would love a mom who can't yell at them when they do wrong."*

He chuckled. "You're going to get your voice back."

She looked down at her lap when she wrote, *"I worry about finding someone who loves me and not the money. If our parents were alive, the inheritance would be far into the future and I could feel more confident."*

Mitch touched her hand and a little charge shot through him.

"What do you do in your spare time when you're at home?"

"Church. Spending time with Simon. Shopping with my girlfriends. You?"

"I'm a big sports fan. I read. And I like to cook."

Her eyes widened.

"I'll have to prepare one of my specialties for you sometime."

"I'd love that."

A big yawn escaped and Ari covered her mouth.

"You should try to get some sleep. It's late and you must be exhausted. I'll check Simon when I do my next walk-around, and I promise to wake you if anything changes."

She nodded and placed the whiteboard and her book on the coffee table.

"Night, Ari."

She waved at Mitch as she lifted her legs onto the sofa and pulled the throw over her.

Back at the other house, Mitch found Tom watching television, his arm wrapped around a bowl of popcorn. "Things okay over there?"

He dropped into the leather armchair. "Ari's not sleeping well. I can't determine if she's protecting her family or suffering from insomnia."

"Probably nightmares. The situation was pretty grim and I'd be willing to bet her need to protect Simon has a lot to do with it. She's always looked out for him."

Mitch considered that.

"Tell me about Simon. You worked for the Kents when he was born?"

"Not much to tell. Michelle Kent went away in early December, came home with the baby in early March and turned him over to Dora. I don't think she wanted another child. Never spent much time with the little guy.

"But then, she's never struck me as the motherly type. She didn't spend a lot of time with Ari either. Hired Dora and then sent Ari off to boarding school after she retired the nanny. Why are you asking about Simon?"

Mitch shrugged. "Ari's made a few comments about their parents that made me wonder."

"The Kents were always on the go. Ari and Simon are blessed to have Dora. She loves them."

Mitch nodded agreement. "Gary's coming in on Sunday for a few days. He's bringing his wife and son. You okay with them staying here?"

Tom shrugged. "Fine with me. The entire downstairs is

open. That should give them plenty of privacy."

Mitch wasn't sure how his sister would react to living with a stranger.

Tom stuffed a handful of popcorn into his mouth and offered the bowl to Mitch.

He shook his head. "Ari says Dora wants to go to Asheville on Sunday to meet her sister and celebrate her birthday. Ari wants one of us to escort her. Means a few days in the lap of luxury. I'd like to stay here with my family, but I'll go if you want."

Tom was silent. After a while, he said, "No. Being your family is coming in, I'll go."

"Thanks, Tom. I promise to keep close watch over Ari and Simon. I told Ari we'd have a cookout on Saturday for Nana's birthday. She's ordered the cake."

"Sounds good. I wield a mean spatula."

"I'm not so bad myself." They watched TV for a while. Mitch looked at his watch. Time to make the rounds again. "I think I'll check on Simon."

"I'm going to finish this movie and see if I can sleep. We've been working such crazy hours that I can't get myself on a normal schedule."

Mitch found the two Kents much as he'd left them. Ari's hair had come loose and curled around her face. Unable to help himself, he brushed back one of the curls and stared at her for a few minutes. She was so beautiful. He picked up the throw that had fallen to the floor and spread it over her. She sighed and shifted on the sofa.

Simon sleepily mumbled his way through the questions, and Mitch left him to his rest before going out to walk the grounds.

❧

The birthday party proved to be fun. As Mitch had said, Simon rebounded and could maneuver himself around the house with a little assistance. The headaches had ceased, and Ari felt comfortable with his recovery.

The two men turned the grilling of the burgers and hot dogs into a competition. When asked to choose the best, Nana declared it a tie and gave each an extra big piece of the birthday cake that had arrived by special delivery that morning.

Ari and Simon's gift was the hotel stay at the Inn on Biltmore Estate along with passes for the Biltmore house and garden for the three of them. There was also a spa day at the Grove Park Inn for the sisters.

"What about you, Tom? Would you like a spa day?" Ari wrote on her whiteboard.

He shook his head. "No, ma'am. I'll drop the ladies off and find something to occupy my time until they finish."

"Ellie will be beside herself," Nana commented. She held up the envelope and eyed Ari. "You know this is way too much."

Ari shook her head and mouthed, *Love you.*

Nana stood and opened her arms. "I love you, too."

Late the next morning they waved Nana and Tom off on their journey. They would return late Thursday afternoon.

"Take care of her," Ari wrote on her board, showing the message to Tom. She had added instructions to have fun for both of them.

Nana looked Mitch straight in the eye. "You take care of my babies."

Tom nodded in agreement.

Mitch smiled and promised he would.

seven

"You already know Gary. This is my sister, Jennifer, and my nephew, William." Mitch lifted the boy from Jen's arms. "Will, meet Ari and Simon."

The baby laughed and waved his arms when Simon made faces at him.

"Hey Will," Simon called. He hopped around behind Mitch with as much agility as anyone sporting a cast could muster, holding on to Mitch's back as he played hide-and-seek with the baby. Will wiggled against his uncle's shoulder, trying to find his new playmate. Simon popped up from the other side and the baby cackled with glee.

Ari rested her hands on Simon's shoulders and shook her head when he glanced up at her.

"It's okay," Mitch said. "Will thinks Simon is great."

Simon grinned broadly.

"I hope you'll come over and play with him this week," Jen invited. "He can't even walk yet and wears me out some days. Heaven help me when he gets older."

"I can't walk good either," Simon said, showing off his casted leg.

"Does it hurt?" Jennifer asked, sounding sympathetic to his plight.

"Itches a lot."

She grimaced. "Yeah, they do. I broke my arm and it itched like crazy."

Gary indicated he wanted to talk to Mitch, so Jennifer took her son from her brother.

The two men strolled over to the edge of the pavement,

looking down over the hill.

"Careful. The trip wire is right there and it's active."

"You'll need to show us where they are so we don't set them off."

He glanced back to where the others stood, Jen talking with Simon and Ari listening and watching baby Will with longing in her eyes. Did Ari want children? There was so much he wanted to know about her. Hard to believe he'd known her for less than a week. "I'll turn them off and we can do it now if you want."

Gary nodded agreement. "I'll show Jen later."

Mitch took care of the system. "Any progress on the case?" he asked as they strolled down the hill.

"They're following leads but nothing yet. Charles and Michelle Kent have powerful friends. They won't let their murders go unsolved. They're also angry over what's happened to Ari and her feeling the need to be in seclusion. The detective says there have been several offers of secure estates with armed guards. Luxury homes."

"Did you tell her?"

Gary nodded. "She says they're fine here. Ari's comfortable with you and Tom. Did you tell her?"

Mitch shook his head. "No. I don't need to muddy up the water with facts."

"Why are you here, Mitch?" Gary asked curiously. "You've never volunteered to assist before."

"Maybe I wanted to be sure nothing happens to my rentals."

Gary shook his head. "You have something on your mind, and I'd like to know what it is."

Mitch glanced at Ari and back to Gary. "I was coming anyway. You know it's all good, don't you? I won't let you down. Nothing is going to happen to them."

"Yeah, I believe that, but I'd still like to know what you're thinking."

Gary wasn't going to let this drop. Mitch supposed his brother-in-law's purpose was twofold—business and personal. "When you first told me how frightened they were, I felt this overwhelming need to do something. Now that I've gotten to know Ari, I find her to be an intriguing, fascinating woman. I wish we'd met outside the current situation."

"The police have talked with everyone from the party. No one recalls seeing anyone who didn't belong."

"Someone does," Mitch said. "Either the killer had help or they need to look for someone with superb climbing skills."

"The last waitstaff to leave has been pinpointed as a person of interest, though the doorman recalls seeing him leave within five minutes of the others."

Gary had made some good connections with the local police over the years and often garnered information when others couldn't.

"Too obvious," Mitch said dismissively.

"I thought so, too. Did you know that lawyer, Langan, lives in the same building as the Kents?"

Mitch's head shot up. He hadn't known.

"Definitely not the penthouse suite, but I suspect he's living above his means. The prices on those places are steep."

"Does the doorman recall any strangers in the building that night?"

"He told the police strangers come and go all the time visiting the tenants."

"Don't they sign in?"

"They call and clear visitors with the residents."

"He also said it appeared Langan and Radnor were arguing when they left that night."

"Wonder what that was about."

"No one knows."

"The answer is right there in our face," Mitch said, instinct telling him all was not as it seemed. "I think Simon being with Ari probably saved his life."

"Me, too," Gary agreed. "Let's finish up here. Jennifer wants to grill out for dinner. Think Ari and Simon would like to join us?"

"I'll ask. She might feel they're intruding and say no."

"We'll have to convince her she's not."

❧

While the men grilled pork chops out on the deck, Ari helped prepare side dishes for the meal. Jennifer insisted they call her Jen.

Ari missed her girlfriends, seeing them at church, getting together to talk or shop. Jen was a great deal of fun and Will was the sweetest baby. She loved his cherubic grins. Simon enjoyed the baby, too. Only thing was his age difference placed him in the role of protector.

After dinner, they all sat around the great room. Simon sat on the floor, his casted leg stretched out to the side as he played with Will on the rug. The cast drew the baby's attention more than the toys Simon offered him.

When her son became fussy, Jen picked him up and announced, "Bedtime for you, little man. I'll be back as soon as I tuck him in."

Simon tried to get up but couldn't. Mitch got up to assist and swung the boy to his feet.

"Will's neat," Simon said as he leaned against the sofa arm and stretched out his leg.

"We like him," Gary agreed. "You want to watch a movie?"

"I checked out the titles already. I've seen all the ones Ari will let me watch."

"We could play games," Jen suggested as she returned to the room. "Thanks, Simon, for helping with Will. He's so tired he could barely keep his eyes open."

Ari smiled at her brother.

"Let's play charades," Mitch suggested. "Ari, Simon, and I

will be a team against you and Gary."

Ari frowned and shook her head. She hated charades.

"Oh come on. It'll be fun," Jen said.

Simon and Mitch put their heads together to come up with clues while Gary and Jen came up with theirs.

"Let her go first," Simon said, pointing to his sister.

Ari pulled a clue from the opposite team's bowl and stared at it for a few moments. One thing was for certain: she wouldn't blurt out the answer. She cupped a hand behind her ear.

"Sounds like," Simon called out. Ari nodded and held up three fingers. Then she made the sign of a movie camera.

"It's a movie," Simon told Mitch.

Ari held up two fingers.

"Second word?"

She pointed out the window toward the lake, stretching her arms outward. Then she moved her arms like she was swimming.

"Swimming," Simon shouted.

She shook her head.

"Water," the boy guessed. Another shake of Ari's head.

"Lake," Mitch called.

Ari smiled and pointed at him, nodding. She held up three fingers.

"Third word?"

Ari held out her arms and looked around the room. Simon and Mitch looked at each other. Ari touched the walls and then the floor.

"House," Simon shouted.

"Something Lake House," Mitch called. "The Lake House."

Ari did a happy dance.

"I told you that clue was too easy," Jen told Gary.

"You never know. Sometimes the most obvious clue is the hardest."

They played until Simon fell asleep on the sofa.

"Come on, buddy," Mitch said, swinging the boy up in his arms for the trip home. "Time for bed. See you guys later."

Ari waved good night and followed Mitch outside. After Simon had been tucked in, Mitch joined Ari for a cup of cocoa. They sat next to each other at the kitchen island.

"Missing Nana?" Mitch asked.

Ari nodded before taking a sip from her mug. She pulled a whiteboard over and wrote, *"She texted me that they arrived safely. I hope they have fun."*

"I'm sure they will." They sat in comfortable silence. Mitch considered this was the way it was with old friends. They didn't need to talk to enjoy each other's company, though he couldn't think of anything he'd like more than to hear her voice. "Ari, tell me about Ann Radnor. When did she work for your father?"

She wrote, *"Years ago. She attends our church. Helps out in Simon's classroom. I've gotten to know her there."*

"What does she look like?"

Ari scribbled, *"Around 5'9", 32 years old. Long dark hair and blue eyes. Why do you ask?"*

"Just wondered. She was at your parents' dinner party."

"She's engaged to Todd Langan."

Mitch read the last comment and thought about how everything linked to the man he wanted to know more about. Why did the doorman think they were arguing? And if they were, why?

"Jen wants to visit the Fields of the Woods Bible Park while she's here, and Gary and I would like to rent a boat and go fishing. Of course our plans depend on whether you and Simon want to come along. If not, we'll hang out here at the house."

"Simon's leg?" Ari wrote on the board.

"I think we can make provisions to get around that. And you might appreciate having others to help entertain him. He'll probably get out of sorts when he can't do what he wants."

Ari shrugged. *"If he's up to it, we'll join your family."*

"Great." Mitch stood. "I'm off to do my walkabout. Call if you need me."

"Come for breakfast," Ari wrote on the whiteboard.

"I'd love to."

Mitch let himself out the downstairs door, whistling softly as he walked the area. He was so glad Jen liked Ari and Simon. He had hoped that would be the case. Of course, his sister was one of those people who never met a stranger and fell into friendships easily.

He thought of Gary's revelation regarding Langan living in the Kents' building. So many things he'd heard seemed to click, but there wasn't a connection that he knew of. Mitch walked down to the dock.

He was standing there when Raquel Wilson came to mind. She had been his patient for nearly six years. Mitch feared her unrelenting anger toward the man who had wronged her would destroy her if she didn't put the situation in the past and move on. Why was he thinking about her now?

Their last session strengthened his feeling that she would never heal emotionally. Tears flowed nonstop as she talked about the man's mistreatment of her. Mitch understood that she would feel wronged. But she hadn't been an innocent. She wasn't so young and naive that she didn't know the price of getting involved with a married man.

He still had no idea who the man was. For six years she had spoken of her experiences without naming one person. While he'd restrained his curiosity when it came to this mystery man, Mitch believed Raquel still loved the man.

Two years before, Raquel hadn't exhibited the excitement of most newly engaged women. She hadn't shared her fiancé's name, set a wedding date, or attempted to show off the large diamond engagement ring Mitch noticed her wearing. He feared for the marriage. At best, he thought she might be settling.

eight

Ari let Mitch in when he arrived early the next morning. He offered to help Simon shower and dress while she worked in the kitchen, putting together their breakfast. After helping Simon settle in his chair, Mitch walked over to the kitchen.

"Anything I can do to help?"

She pointed to the plates of bacon and eggs. Ari picked up the plate of toast and paused to remove a pitcher of orange juice from the fridge. The honey butter and jam were on the table. After Simon said grace, they began to eat.

"We were thinking of renting a pontoon boat and going fishing today." Mitch shook out his napkin and placed it in his lap. "You interested or would you prefer to hang out here?"

Ari wasn't sure about spending the day with them but could see the longing in Simon's expression and gave in to his pleas. She had dressed in shorts and a sleeveless top and slid her feet into a pair of backless sneakers.

Mitch cleaned the kitchen while she made preparations for their outing. After rubbing sunscreen on her arms and face, she packed a carryall with the items they would need, including her whiteboard and marker. A safari straw hat would shield her face from the sun. She handed Simon a baseball cap and sunshades and put on her own sunglasses. She added snack items and indicated she was ready to go. Simon moved in front of her, swinging along on his crutches.

They met the Bishops at the vehicle and drove over to the marina. The men quickly made the arrangements to rent the boat and bought bait. They filled a large cooler with ice for their catch and another smaller one with ice, sodas, and water. Gary asked someone from the marina to help them rig a shade canopy to protect the baby from the late August sun's strong rays.

Jen stepped onto the pontoon boat and settled herself and Will underneath the canopy. Mitch carried Simon on board and sat him up front before going back to help Gary with the rest of their gear.

Ari chose a seat near Jen. She rooted around in her bag and tossed Simon the tube of sunscreen. He rubbed it onto his face, arms, and one bare leg and then lobbed it back.

She offered it to Jen, who read the label and smeared some over Will's exposed body. "Thanks for reminding me. I was going to pick up a tube and forgot."

Ari pointed to Jen's arms, indicating she should use the sunscreen as well.

When Mitch stepped onto the boat, Ari offered him the tube. He wore shorts, a worn T-shirt, and an old fishing hat, lures of all kinds hanging from the brim.

"Thanks." He grinned and flipped open the cap, rubbing the lotion onto his face and arms. With his darker complexion she doubted he'd burn as easily as her and Simon with their fair skin. She nodded toward Gary, and Mitch passed the tube on.

"Okay, now that everyone is properly protected," Mitch said with a teasing glance in Ari's direction, "I think we're ready to cast off."

He expertly slid the boat from the berth and moved out into the open water, going slowly through the wake. Ari noted the ease with which he handled the boat. He'd done this before.

Ari truly appreciated Mitch. Handsome, kind, and considerate were major adjectives that described him in her book. Plus he always seemed to know what to say to comfort her when she felt depressed.

She remembered the way he'd comforted her after Simon's accident and blushed slightly. Ari liked the feeling of being in his arms, and the soothing timbre of his voice was something she could listen to forever.

"So what do you think of my big brother?"

There was a definite twinkle in Jen's brown gaze when she shot her brother a cheeky grin. Ari pulled out her board and a marker. *He's been a great help to Simon and me.*

"That's good. Generally he makes a pest of himself." Mitch made a face at Jen, and she retaliated by sticking out her tongue. Her expression changed to one of sadness. "Actually, I'm thankful he's here for you both. I know it's a difficult time. I'm praying."

Ari mouthed, *Thank you.*

"Mitch tells me you're a believer, too." She settled her son in her lap and leaned back in the seat. "I don't know how people make it through without Jesus to lean on in times like this. I was ten when we lost our parents in a fire. Mitch was thirteen. He got burned in the fire and was in the hospital for a long time. We went to stay with Mom's sister. I love Aunt Sandy, but she wasn't Mom or Dad. She didn't know our special things. It was hard, and I cried myself to sleep for weeks."

Ari had witnessed the scars left behind by the fire. Mitch said he nearly died but hadn't mentioned his parents. Why hadn't he told her? Surely he understood what she'd been feeling. He'd been the older sibling, too.

She understood the sudden loss of all you held near and dear. While families often seemed to take each other for granted, losing key members changed everything. "Don't get me wrong. I know we were blessed to have a place to go and someone who loved us. Aunt Sandy is like a grandmother to Will. He adores her." Jen's gaze filled with love as she glanced down at the baby in her lap. "She keeps him while I work." Jen noted Ari's interest and said, "I help Gary at the office for a few hours each day."

"She's quite the detective." From his seat at the front of the boat, Gary shared a private smile with his wife. His right eye closed in a playful wink. "My sweet, sweet computer expert. Need a background check or a missing person found, call Jen."

The look of love that passed between husband and wife gave Ari a bittersweet feeling. Would she ever find that special person who looked at her with that much love? She hoped so.

"That's how we met." Jen's gaze rested on her husband. "Mitch worked for Gary's dad and asked if they had something part-time for me."

Mitch thumped Gary's shoulder. "And you fell right into trouble's open arms."

"Hey, watch it." Gary took a step back to catch his balance.

Jen chuckled. "Aunt Sandy worried about me spending too much time on the computer. Gary taught me how to put it to good use. If it's out there, I can find it."

"Maybe the police can hire you to find out who killed our mom and dad."

Four sets of adult eyes rested on the child's forlorn expression. *If only it were that easy,* Ari thought.

Mitch patted Simon's shoulder.

"I'm sure they're looking as hard as they can," Jen told Simon.

"The police won't stop looking until they find them," Gary added.

Unconvinced, Simon shrugged.

Ari's phone beeped. She mouthed, *Excuse me,* and clicked on the e-mail to find a message forwarded by Shannon. She scowled as she read through yet another of Todd Langan's demanding e-mails.

"Something wrong?" Jen asked.

Ari shook her head. She wasn't about to ruin everyone's day with her problems. Her gaze drifted to where Simon sat at the wheel listening as Mitch showed him how to drive the boat.

The child's frequent questioning glances in Mitch's direction showed his eagerness to please. Mitch rewarded him with a big grin and another pat on the shoulder. Simon beamed with happiness.

Ari considered how different their father had been. Charles Kent wasn't the type to heap compliments on anyone's head. If you performed well, it was no more and no less than he expected. Fail and suffer his wrath. She knew. She'd failed a time or two.

He hadn't kicked her out of the family, but he'd treated her exactly like his other employees. She had reprimand letters in her personnel file to prove she'd let him down. It occurred to Ari that she should do away with them now that she was the boss. No, they would remain to serve as a reminder not to let herself or her parents down in the future.

What would Simon's adult relationship with his father have been like? Would he have been more understanding of his son? More tolerant? Or tougher?

Ari guessed their father would have demanded more of Simon. Even at a young age, the boy had more activities than most kids. Dad probably thought Simon would carry on the family business. She knew her father believed she would marry, have children, and lose interest, but Ari loved her work and intended to find a way to merge business and family in a mutually satisfactory way.

As they moved farther onto the lake, Ari noted the shadows cast by the trees that surrounded the large expanse of water. She felt hopelessly lost in the vastness of the lake.

Mitch pointed up the hill. "There's your house."

That caught Ari's attention. How had he found his way here? She was hopeless when it came to navigating. Even Chicago where she had lived most of her life.

Mitch turned the boat in a wide swath and headed back out into the lake. After a while, he shut down the engine and allowed the boat to float.

"Are we going to fish now?" Simon asked, his voice filled with childish excitement.

"Yep." Mitch settled the boy in a seat near the bow and pulled a cooler over to serve as a leg prop. He added an extra life jacket as a cushion. "Comfortable?"

Simon nodded. Mitch had come over the day before and they'd assembled the spinning rod. Now he demonstrated how it worked.

"You take care of your rods, and they'll serve you forever. I have some my dad owned. He took me fishing when I was your age. Those were some of the best times of my life."

The boy's eyes widened. "Really, your dad took you?"

Ari paid close attention to their exchange, hoping Mitch wouldn't make promises he wouldn't keep.

"He did. We went on father-son fishing trips a couple of times a year. He taught me everything his dad taught him."

"Will you teach me what your dad taught you?"

"You bet."

"The rods and Daddy's fishing boat were in a building behind our house," Jen told Ari as they witnessed the exchange between the man and boy. "Aunt Sandy had to sell the boat, but she kept the rods for Mitch."

I'm sure he treasures them," Ari wrote.

Jen nodded. "One day Mitch and Gary will use them to teach Will like they're doing for Simon now." A tear leaked out and ran along her smooth cheek. "I'm glad he has this little piece of our dad to hold on to. Something he can pass on to his son. I wish he could find someone and settle down.

Though I don't know how he'll ever meet anyone. He works way too many hours."

Ari considered Mitch's interaction with Simon. He'd make a good father. A good husband for that matter. Obviously a hard worker and dedicated to taking care of his security company assignments, he'd be a good provider. It surprised her that he hadn't been snapped up long before now.

Mitch reached into the box he'd picked up at the marina and demonstrated for Simon the technique of baiting the hook. "You can do this next time."

She couldn't look.

The boat floated on the currents. Everyone talked softly. Ari felt like a very minute part of a much bigger world.

"I've got something," Simon yelled, jarring the peacefulness.

"Let's see."

Mitch stood behind the boy's shoulder and directed, reaching out to net his catch. Simon's fish was a striped bass about ten inches long.

"Wicked," he declared in a long, breathless cry. "Ari, look. I caught a fish."

She smiled. Jen snapped a picture of him holding his first catch. Gary offered his hand in a high five.

Mitch slid the fish into the cooler and reached for the bait container. Ari closed her eyes again as Simon worked it onto the hook without doing harm to himself. Once more Mitch demonstrated how to cast the line back into the water.

"Come on, Gare," Mitch said with a grin. "We can't let this newbie outfish us."

Simon swept out his arms, the pole clutched in one hand. "This big," he said with a pleased giggle.

"You'd better hold on with both hands in case that monster comes looking for you," Mitch said.

Jen spread a blanket on the bottom of the boat and slipped down to play with Will. Ari had missed most of this stage with Simon and found it intriguing. The baby turned and twisted in all directions, rolling from his back to his stomach.

Occasionally he sat up without his mother's support. He inched across the blanket to the toys out of his reach and reached for those she dangled. Will babbled as he moved his toys from one hand to the other and looked at his mom when she called his name. When he started to cry, she slipped a pacifier into his mouth.

Jen was a good mother, Ari thought. Caring and capable, her love for her child obvious in the way she handled him. He grinned as he stood on tiptoes and bounced in her lap.

When Ari held out her arms, Will jumped at her.

"Hold on tight," Jen told her. "He's a wiggly one."

Ari considered that she could communicate on the baby's level. Would the others understand her cries if she reverted to the alarms of infancy?

She lifted his shirt and blew a raspberry against his soft stomach. Will laughed and reared back in her arms.

Mitch glanced over at them and said, "Check out Will over there hanging out with the pretty girls."

"Yeah, my boy's quite the ladies' man," Gary said with fatherly pride.

"Not so hard to get attention at that age," Mitch said.

"Don't be a hater," Jen called.

Mitch laughed and said, "Okay, so Will and I need to talk. Maybe he can give his old uncle a few tips."

Everyone laughed. Maybe Will could give her some tips, Ari thought wryly.

They fished on. The sun moved in the sky. Half a dozen catches later, Jen wiped away the fine beads of sweat clinging to her forehead and said, "It's time to cruise for a bit. It's hot sitting in one place."

Mitch dropped a largemouth bass into the cooler. "Okay. We have enough fish for dinner anyway. Simon, looks like you have the biggest catch of the day."

"I do?"

Mitch nodded. "Now you get to learn how to clean a fish."

"You mean like give it a bath?"

"No, like take off the scales and gut it. Get it ready to cook and eat."

Simon grimaced and cried, "Ewww."

"It's not so bad. Remember what I told you. We eat what we catch. You'll be glad once they're cooked. Fish have all sorts of health benefits. They are great brain food."

"You should eat—" Jen began.

"Don't say it," Mitch warned, pointing a finger at her.

Her slow grin indicated he was no threat to her. "A whale."

"You'll pay for that. What do you think, Simon? Should I toss her overboard?"

"No, Mitch. Will would be sad without his mom."

"Okay, Jen, thank Simon for your reprieve."

She took a couple of steps forward and kissed Simon's cheek before she thumped Mitch's head.

"Ouch. You bully. Go sit down before I change my mind." He nudged Simon and said, "We get to use knives."

"Ari won't let me have a knife."

He frowned. "Yeah, I suppose you are a little young for that. We'll try you on the scaler. I'll show you how it's done. Then when you're older and go camping, you'll be able to prepare and cook your catch."

Jen passed around sodas and snacks to everyone. They ate and stayed out on the water for another hour before calling it a day. Back at the marina, they cleaned off the boat and headed for their vehicle.

At home, Jen took Will inside for a nap. Mitch, Gary, and Simon made quick work of cleaning the fish and put them in the fridge.

"We'll fry these," Mitch said. "I need to make a grocery

run. Gary will be here."

Ari had showered and changed into clean clothes. Her wet hair hung down her back. She held up the whiteboard. *"We'll ride with you."*

He glanced at Gary and shrugged. Gary went home, and Mitch helped Simon shower after wrapping his leg in a plastic trash bag and securing it with tape. After Simon was dressed, they accompanied Mitch over to the other house to wait while he did the same.

"Simon could hang out with us at the pool," Jen said. "He could stick one leg in the water."

Simon thumped his cast. "I can't swim or do nothing with this stupid thing."

Mitch came into the room, dressed in worn jeans and a T-shirt bearing the Bishop Security logo.

"They make waterproof cast protectors. We need to find a medical supply store. Get you one for the shower, too. Easier than rigging plastic bags and tape."

Simon's eyes widened. "Really? They make those?" He turned to look at her. "Hey, Ari, can we find one? Please?"

She glanced at Mitch.

"Let's check the phone book," he said. "If they don't have them locally, we'll get one overnighted. Think you can wait another day, Simon?"

He nodded enthusiastically. "If it means I can go swimming again before the end of the summer."

Mitch called around and found the item in Murphy. Simon decided to stay with the Bishops. Ari went with Mitch. At the store, they decided on a couple of cast protectors and paid for them with the company card.

"You never know what they'll come up with next," the salesclerk said as she dropped the items and receipt into a bag.

"This is going to make one little boy very happy." He glanced at Ari and they shared a smile.

After a trip to the grocery store for fresh cabbage, cornmeal for hush puppies, batter mix, and a couple of other items, they picked up the mail. Mitch drove toward home as Ari reviewed the correspondence that had been forwarded.

"Something wrong?" Mitch asked when she glanced at him.

Ari didn't know what to make of the letter. Back at the house, she handed the sheet of stationery to Mitch and watched as he read the personal note from a board member's wife.

"Ari, dear," Eileen Reynolds wrote. *"I've returned home from Paris and must tell you I'm very troubled by all that's happened to your family in my absence. If there is anything I can do to assist you, please let me know. Perhaps it is wise to put someone in an acting managerial role until you get your voice back. You poor thing. This is so terrible."*

He handed it back. "What does she mean by put someone in an acting role? Has anyone said anything to you about doing that? What's going on?"

Ari shrugged and reached for her whiteboard. *"First I've heard of it."*

"Mind if I share this with Gary?"

She shook her head.

&

"Something's going on in Chicago," Mitch told Gary as they fried up the fish that evening.

He had planned an old-fashioned fish fry for dinner. The coleslaw was made and chilling in the fridge, and he would start dropping the hush puppies in hot oil shortly. "Ari got this letter from a board member's wife." He handed it over.

Gary read and demanded, "What does she mean about assigning someone in an acting managerial role? Ari's not having any problems managing things from here."

"Someone's up to no good. Think the husband knows the wife spilled the beans?"

"I doubt it," Gary said. "She probably doesn't even realize it's a covert operation."

"I'd like to know who they're proposing for the takeover."

Gary appeared thoughtful. "We need to find out. How's Ari taking the news?"

"She's as confused as we are."

"I'll make some calls in the morning."

Mitch doubted Ari would wait that long to learn what was going on.

❧

Inside, Ari sat at the dining table with her laptop, reading Shannon's comment over and over.

SCrown: *I did hear a rumor the board plans to put an acting chief executive officer in place until you're able to resume your full-time duties. I wanted verification before I told you. There's been so much garbage regarding the company floating around.*

Ari stared at the screen. No doubt the board was worried, but they had even less to lose in all this than she and Simon did. Why wouldn't they attempt to contact her with their concerns? All they had to do was send an e-mail to the hotel. Todd Langan should have told her in one of his many e-mails.

AKent: *Any idea who's involved?*

SCrown: *I've heard Todd Langan's name mentioned in connection to Kent more than once. I've taken to recording his calls. He's threatening me. I've been meaning to forward his last one.*

AKent: *I will be at the next board meeting. Eileen Reynolds sent a note in that last batch of mail. I don't think her husband intended for her to share the news, but apparently what you've heard is true. They're up to something and I want to know what it is.*

SCrown: *What do you need to be able to communicate in the boardroom?*

AKent: *Laptop, projector and screen.*

SCrown: *I'll make sure they're available. When will you arrive? Will you stay at your townhouse?*

AKent: *No. Book two rooms with connecting doors and another single room across the hall. Put the rooms in Gary Bishop's name.*

SCrown: *I'll handle it myself.*

AKent: *Thanks, Shannon.*

Ari printed the screen and signed off the IM program.

A few seconds later, the forwarded voice message clicked onto her phone. She turned up the volume to listen.

"This is Todd Langan. I need to speak to Arianna Kent immediately."

"I'm sorry, Mr. Langan, but as I've told you many times, Ms. Kent is unavailable."

"Where is she?" he demanded. "She needs to be here. The police would be more productive if she were present, pushing them to investigate. The board needs to know what she plans to do. This is ridiculous. I am her lawyer."

His gruff, angry tone infuriated Ari.

Shannon's voice came over the phone. "Ari will be in touch when she's ready. Meanwhile, I'm sure the police are doing everything they can. And surely the board understands how traumatic this is for her and Simon?"

He snorted. "I don't think you're forwarding my messages to Ms. Kent. In fact, I plan to discuss your attitude with her."

"You do that, Mr. Langan. Have a nice day."

Ari laughed, cheering silently when Shannon hung up on the man. She didn't need this sneak representing her. Sure, she'd been out of contact, but there was no reason for him to attempt a coup. It was time she showed Mr. Langan who was in charge.

She turned to the laptop and typed a memo to Erik George, the law firm's senior partner, requesting a private meeting early Thursday morning to discuss replacing Todd Langan as counsel for Kent Enterprises. She also requested his presence at the next board meeting.

A thought occurred and Ari texted another message to Shannon. PLEASE NOTIFY ALL SENIOR STAFF THAT MY PRESENCE IS TO BE KEPT UNDER WRAPS. I DON'T WANT THE PRESS OR ANYONE ELSE KNOWING I'M IN CHICAGO.

WHAT WILL YOU WEAR?

Clothes. She hadn't planned that far yet. There certainly weren't any power suits in her wardrobe here.

PLEASE RUN BY MY APARTMENT AND PICK UP MY BLACK SILK AND THE NEW NAVY SUIT. IT'S STILL IN THE GARMENT BAG. CHOOSE SOME BLOUSES AND BRING MY FERRAGAMO PUMPS. THANKS, SHANNON.

I'M PRAYING, ARI.

PLEASE KEEP IT UP. KNOWING THAT GOD'S LOVE SURROUNDS ME MAKES LIFE BEARABLE RIGHT NOW.

Ari turned off the computer and walked out onto the deck.

Mitch glanced up. "Gary and I were discussing the note. He'll do some follow-up tomorrow morning."

No need, Ari wrote on the whiteboard. *I've verified that there is a rumor and suspect something is planned for the next board meeting. I need to be there."*

Gary nodded. "Let's meet after dinner to discuss the particulars."

Not hungry, Ari managed a few bites of the tasty fish before putting down her fork. Simon's enthusiasm over his role of provider in the meal was obvious. Afterward Ari helped clean up and load the dishwasher. Jen took Will and went downstairs with Simon to check out the playroom.

"You want to meet in here or on the deck?" Mitch asked.

She pointed toward the living room.

They settled on the sofa and armchairs. Ari held her whiteboard and marker.

Gary took a pad of paper and pen from his shirt pocket. "You want the same amount of security you have here or more?"

She wrote on the board and held it up for him to read. *"Nana and Simon will remain in North Carolina with Tom. You and Mitch will travel with me."*

"That's good," Gary said. "We can keep a closer watch on you without worrying about them. Jen plans to stay here while we're gone. She'll help Nana with Simon. I can bring in more people if you feel the need."

"Tell her to come here and stay. Nana will enjoy spoiling your son rotten," Ari wrote, grinning as she held up the board again for Gary to read. She swiped it clean with her palm and jotted the plans for their hotel stay.

Gary whistled. "If you're ever in need of a job, let me know. I need people as thorough as you in my business."

She swiped again and wrote, *"Let's see what happens at the board meeting. If they divest me of my job, I may take you up on the offer. Oh, there's more."*

Ari took out her phone and played the call for them.

"You think Langan's behind this?" Mitch asked.

She wrote, *"I do. I've contacted Erik George and requested a private meeting Thursday morning to discuss removing Langan as counsel for the company. I have no idea what Todd Langan's agenda is, but he's not going to succeed."*

"When is the board meeting?"

She scribbled on the board and flipped it up for them to view. *"Next Thursday at 10 a.m. Before then, I want to meet with staff and the attorney and familiarize myself with everything that's happened since Daddy's death. I want to leave late Monday afternoon so we don't arrive in Chicago too early. Shannon will notify the hotel management staff of my presence but it will not be made public."*

"I'll make the flight arrangements," Gary said.

nine

Later that night, Ari rocked on the balcony, her thoughts on the future and what their parents' deaths meant to her and Simon. The most difficult thing for her was knowing they wouldn't be there when she needed them most. Her dad would have known what to do. The board would never try something like this with him. Ari knew she had to take a stand now if she hoped to maintain control in the future.

The changes she'd made in her life since college had been difficult for everyone to understand, particularly her parents. They couldn't comprehend why church was more important than the other activities they felt she should be enjoying at her age. Nor had she been interested in the men they often sent her way.

Ari knew her beliefs would have a major impact on her management role within the company. Already she prayed continuously over the operation of her one hotel, and she could see herself praying around the clock with the added corporate responsibilities.

She had to do what was right. And her promise to God was to do it in a Christian way. Still, the information she'd learned today made her angry. They had no right. She and Simon had lost so much. And to know members of the board questioned her ability hurt.

Ari knew economic changes made investors more cautious, but she also knew without doubt that not one detail in the day-to-day operations had been left unhandled.

Even though Charles Kent was no longer with them, his legacy was a system that assured business as usual in his absence. Not one man or woman he'd chosen would willingly allow a negative to reflect badly on them or the company.

Having her in the chair behind the desk or at the table in the boardroom was not going to change anything. She would continue to depend on their staff. She had not remained idle here in the mountains. Ari communicated with corporate staff on a daily basis. She'd also read and responded to every document she'd been sent. Every member of her staff could testify that she'd been hands-on even at a distance.

Ari considered what returning to Chicago and the requirements of the job would mean to her and Simon. No matter how demanding the situation, she had to be certain he knew she was there for him when he needed her.

"You okay?" Mitch's greeting was a husky whisper.

So lost in thought she hadn't heard him climbing the stairs, Ari let out a little scream. He had pulled on a navy windbreaker since dinner, making him nearly invisible in the dark. She took the phone from her lap and typed, *"Have I done the right thing by staying away?"*

"Why would you ask that?"

She typed, *"Ann Radnor e-mailed that the church is praying for us and wants me to contact her and let her know we're okay. I don't even know her that well."*

"Isn't she Langan's fiancée?"

Ari nodded.

"You think she's trying to get in touch with you for Langan?"

Ari nodded again.

"These people can't even begin to understand what you're going through, and for them to try to pressure you now is wrong."

"What if my presence would make the police work harder?"

Mitch read and shook his head. "Gary already told you the police are under a great deal of pressure. I think it's safe to say you have sufficient representation in Chicago to keep the police on the case. But even without the pressure, they want to find this person as much as you want them found. If you were there, they would have to protect you and Simon."

She considered what he'd said and accepted it was true.

"You aren't worried about this trip, are you?" he asked.

Ari picked up her phone and typed, *"Trying to think things through."*

"And finding it harder because you're feeling betrayed?"

Jesus and Judas. Ari knew her situation didn't begin to compare, but she did feel wronged. Her fingers moved on the keyboard. *"Why can't they give me time?"*

The light from the phone illuminated her sad expression before she turned it in his direction.

"Someone has gotten into their heads and convinced them they can't afford to delay. No doubt they're receiving the same amount of information, but they let their doubts force them to take action because there's not a Kent behind the big desk."

Mitch sat down next to her and took her hand in his. Ari welcomed the comfort of his touch and the familiarity of their midnight routine. Her inability to speak didn't seem to matter.

"Your hand is cold," Mitch said, raising it to his lips. The warmth of his breath against her skin felt nice. He kissed her hand.

She drank in the comfort of his nearness, wishing for more.

"My guess is they're as afraid of what's going to happen as you are," he said with quiet emphasis.

"Different reasons perhaps, but this nightmare affected them in different ways. For one thing, you can be sure they're considering their own security in a world gone crazy. A couple they trusted and liked is dead and their murderer is out there on the streets.

"Who knows, maybe they consider it a kindness to lift the burden from your shoulders. They probably don't realize they're doing you a great injustice and causing you unnecessary pain with their actions."

"You should be a counselor," Ari typed.

He moved restlessly, releasing her hand. "What's your biggest concern? What you fear could happen to you and Simon? Or what will happen with the company?"

"Simon," Ari wrote.

"Don't worry. Gary and I will be there making sure you're safe. Tom and Jen will be here looking after Simon and Nana. And while Jen might look like an innocent, my sister has her own pistol and can outshoot the trainers at the range."

Ari could see Jen taking on the bad guys. She smiled. *"I'm not worried,"* she typed. *"God is in control. I've asked Him to cast a net of safety over us all."*

"The police are going to find this person, Ari. Sooner or later, someone will slip up, and when they do, they'll be caught."

They sat in silence, studying the huge moon hanging over the water. It was almost as bright as daylight out here.

"Jen wants to go to the Fields of the Wood Bible Park tomorrow. You okay with that?"

Ari nodded. She'd read about it in the brochure she'd picked up at the tourism center and decided it would be an interesting place to visit. The sudden wail of the alarm made the hairs on her arms stand at attention.

Mitch jumped into action. "Get inside. Now. Lock the door."

Ari froze. His no-nonsense tone made her heart pound in rhythm with the loud bleat. When she didn't move, he opened the door and pushed her inside.

❧

The need to protect her overwhelmed Mitch. He pressed the

TALK button on the phone, calling Gary. "I'm on the deck at the other house. Someone set off the alarm. Looks like a boat down at the dock."

Gary's clipped tone ordered, "Stay with Ari and Simon. I'll check it out."

In the distance, Mitch heard voices, saw the three men who had climbed out of their boat. Their voices carried in the night air as an argument ensued.

"You idiot. This isn't our dock."

"Looks like our dock," the man muttered.

"You said you knew where you were going."

A couple of minutes later, the alarm stopped and Mitch spotted the flashlight as Gary jogged down the hill. He'd break his leg if he didn't slow down.

He shouted, "You're trespassing on private property."

"Hey man," one guy objected, holding up his hands and taking a step back on the dock. He nearly fell over the edge. The others grabbed him. "We got lost. Came in at the wrong inlet."

"Then I'd suggest you move this party along before we call the police."

"Police? Hey man, no foul. We were having fun."

"Probably best to have your fun during daylight hours without the aid of alcohol. Deep water in this lake. No one would ever find you if you fell overboard."

"What do you mean by that?" another man slurred.

Mitch took a step forward on the deck, feeling as Simon must have felt that first day. There was no way he could get down there in time if these men jumped Gary. Did he have his gun?

"No foul, man," Gary countered somewhat sarcastically. "You've obviously had too much to drink to find your way home."

"Don't antagonize them, Gary," Mitch mumbled under his breath.

"We're good. We're right around there," the man said, pointing in the opposite direction. Then he frowned and turned to point the other way. "Or maybe there."

He noted Gary kept a good distance between himself and the men.

"I suggest you get back in the boat and get out of here now."

They started to move away. One of them stopped and demanded, "Hey, who's staying up there? Must be someone important to have these noisemakers."

"No one you'd know," Gary said. "You should get out of here before my partner summons the police. He's armed. My wife is on the other deck and she's an even better shot."

They all but jumped from the dock into the boat.

The motor started up after a few tries and they rode off into the vastness of Lake Hiwassee.

"All clear," Gary said into the radio. "Idiots got lost on the lake. Thought they were on their dock. I'll watch for a while to make sure they don't double back, and I'll reset the alarms. Might be wise to notify the guardhouse before they call the police."

"Will do."

Mitch dialed the guardhouse and explained what had happened.

"Thanks," the man told him. "Maybe I should give the fish and game people a call. We don't need those idiots out there frightening people."

"Might be a good idea for their safety as well," Mitch agreed as he opened the door and stepped inside.

Ari huddled on the sofa, Simon hugged close to her. His crutches rested against the chair arm. Mitch knelt before them. He touched Simon's arm. "You okay, buddy?"

The child appeared anxious. "Who was it? Why did they come on our dock?"

"They were lost. Gary's watching to make sure they're

gone. Think you can go back to sleep?"

Simon snuggled closer to Ari. "Maybe I'll stay here on the couch for a while."

"Okay. You want something to drink? I make pretty good cocoa."

Simon nodded. Mitch looked at Ari. "What about you?"

She followed him to the kitchen. They took out milk and a bottle of chocolate syrup and heated the milk on the stove.

"Not the traditional recipe," Mitch said as he stirred to keep the milk from scorching. "But it will do for tonight. That alarm scared ten years off my life."

Ari reached for a whiteboard and wrote, *"Mine, too."*

She produced a bag of marshmallows and floated two in each cup. They took their mugs into the living room and sipped the hot chocolate, the warmth helping to chase away the anxiety.

Several minutes later, Simon struggled to keep his eyes open.

"Think you can sleep now?" Mitch asked.

The boy nodded and reached for his crutches.

When Ari stood to help Simon, Mitch caught her hand and squeezed reassuringly. "I won't let anything happen to either of you."

Ari smiled her thanks.

The radio chirped. "All clear," Gary said. "They're still fumbling around out there. Probably try every inlet between here and Murphy."

"They may get a visitor. You think they'll return?"

"Maybe out of curiosity, but with any luck, they'll forget their way back. They know about the alarms now. I'm headed back up to the house. Jen and Will are probably already asleep."

"I thought she was on the deck," Mitch said.

Gary laughed. "Messing with their heads."

Mitch chuckled. He followed Ari and Simon into the sunroom and helped Simon settle on the sofa bed.

He shifted in the bed and winced. "My leg hurts tonight. Can I have something for the pain?"

Ari nodded and left the room.

"Are those guys really gone, Mitch?"

He nodded. "Gary says they're out there on the lake trying to find their way home. How bad is your leg?"

Simon shrugged. "Cast feels really tight."

Mitch turned back the cover and probed his foot and upper thigh. "Your leg is swelling. Let's prop it a little higher." He stacked two more pillows under the casted leg. "Comfortable?"

Simon nodded.

Mitch sat on the side of the bed. "You did really well for your first time fishing. We'll have to go out again soon."

Simon grinned with pleasure. "I like fishing. When you first told me about it, it didn't sound like fun, but it was."

"Told you." Mitch grinned and patted his shoulder.

Ari returned with the medication and water, and Mitch left them alone. After a while, she came back into the living room and curled up on the leather sofa, wrapping herself in a chenille throw. The silence stretched on for several minutes. "What's on your mind?" he asked finally.

She shrugged, looking despondent.

"Everything's okay. They were drunk and lost."

She reached for the whiteboard. *"No. It's not. I'm sick of scurrying off to hide."*

"Sometimes it's wise to be afraid."

After a derisive look, she wrote furiously, *"Not if I'm afraid of my own shadow. Tonight a group of innocent strangers put me in a panic. I let the fear break through my shield of faith. I became afraid and ran for my life. I didn't trust God and now I can't stop running."*

Mitch thought about trusting God. Ari had done what she had to do. She'd moved herself out of harm's way. Surely this was God's plan to keep her safe. "This other situation has you on edge. I wish I knew what that lawyer thinks he's doing."

The near fury in his tone flabbergasted her.

Ari swiped the board clean and wrote, *"Nothing makes sense."*

"You're tired. Go to bed. Try to sleep. You'll feel better in the morning."

She shook her head and wrote, *"I can't live like this, Mitch. I have to take back control of my life."*

"You will. Meanwhile, I'm here, Ari. Keeping watch over you and Simon. Sleep, and then tomorrow you can concentrate on this situation with the board."

She nodded.

Mitch secured the house and went outside to start his patrol.

"Sleep well, sweetheart," he whispered a few minutes later when her bedroom light flashed off.

Mitch thought of Ari's comment about his being a good counselor. He knew he should tell her the truth, but for now, it was more important to keep her safe. He didn't even realize what he was doing when he prayed the remainder of the night would pass in silence and that God would give Ari comfort. She surely needed it now.

ten

Ari let Mitch in when he arrived around nine thirty the following morning. Simon sat at the table eating a bowl of cereal.

"Good morning. Figured you wouldn't mind sleeping in. You up to sightseeing today?" he asked cheerfully.

Ari picked up the whiteboard and scribbled, *"What about those men? Will they come back?"*

Mitch kept his voice low as he said, "The alarms worked, Ari, and they'll continue to work. Did you sleep at all last night?"

She shrugged and he knew she hadn't. She scribbled on the whiteboard and held it up. "Probably as much as you."

"Gary covered me for a few hours this morning. Would you feel safer somewhere else?"

Ari shook her head. *"I have to take a stand or I'll be running for the rest of my life. I have to trust God to take care of us."*

"We'll make sure you're safe," Mitch said.

"He will, you know. He's already blessed us with you, Gary, and Tom," Ari wrote.

Mitch felt uncomfortable with the idea that she saw him as some kind of guardian angel sent by God. He was just a man and not always proud of his actions.

"Are you too tired for Fields of the Wood today?"

She shook her head.

"Okay then, let's go. It'll do you good to have something else to occupy your mind for a while."

The day was overcast.

"Rain?" Jen asked when they gathered at the SUV.

"We've had beautiful weather up until now," Mitch said, leaving her to draw her own conclusions.

Jen punched his arm. "There's no rain cloud over my head."

"Grab your raincoat and let's go. You won't melt."

Gary greeted Ari and Simon. "You doing okay after that scare last night? Mitch said you're worried. Don't be. I doubt they could find their way back."

"I thought I was going to have to come downstairs to help you," Mitch said.

"If they'd intended harm, I'd have been toast by the time you made it down those stairs. You need a zip line off that deck. Or an elevator.

"That's why I live in the city," Gary continued. "I'm a big fan of elevators."

"He wants to put one in our house," Jen said. "I told him he's crazy. It's two floors. Between the remote and an elevator, he'd never get any exercise."

"I get plenty of exercise," Gary objected.

"Yeah, to and from the elevator in your office building," Jen teased. "One of these days you're going to get stuck in one, and then we'll see how you feel about them."

Fields of the Wood Bible Park was down the road from where they were staying. Mitch drove, and when he passed through the white archway, they were all pleasantly surprised. Earlier Mitch had asked Jen to help him cheer up Ari and Simon. She'd appointed herself tour guide for the trip and brought along the information she'd printed off. His sister never went anywhere without a computer and collected electronics like most women collected jewelry.

"Says the park was built in 1945 by the Church of God of Prophecy and there's over two hundred acres," Jen read from her papers.

"Those are the world's largest Ten Commandments. Three hundred feet wide with five-foot-tall letters and three hundred fifty steps between the tablets."

Everyone looked toward the display featured on the

mountainside. Mitch let out an impressed whistle. Simon followed suit.

Gary groaned. "More steps."

Her husband's reaction prompted Jen to add, "And you can climb up inside the Bible at the top."

Mitch parked and everyone but Will climbed out of the vehicle. The baby slept peacefully in his car seat. Ari motioned for them to pose and lifted her phone to snap a photo with the backdrop of God's laws spelled out on the grassy hillside.

Mitch pointed to the right. "There's the service road. If you three want to climb up Ten Commandment Mountain, Simon, Will, and I can meet you up top."

"I'm willing if you are," Jen told Ari.

"Hey, wait a minute—that means I have to walk with you," Gary said. He eyed his brother-in-law suspiciously. "I'm onto you, buddy."

Mitch's innocent and slightly offended expression didn't fool anyone as he said, "Your wife thinks you need exercise, and I offered to babysit your son."

Gary gave Mitch the evil eye. "Okay, ladies," he said, offering them his arms, "shall we go for a stroll?"

Jen and Ari shared a smile as they stepped forward. Mitch didn't fool anyone with his plan. He'd never intended to climb the mountain.

The feeling of oneness with God returned as Ari read the commandments.

Jen appeared at her elbow. "This place is wonderful. I feel that way every time I come here. Can you believe the detail? Someone spent a lot of time getting it right."

Every time? Ari wondered how often the Bishops visited the area. Maybe they knew the owner of the houses. Gary had come up with the safe houses relatively quickly.

Ari agreed with Jen. She wouldn't mind coming back. If

only she could voice her feelings. She was overwhelmed by the love and dedication that had created this wonderful site.

Jen and Gary moved on ahead, reading the commandments aloud as they climbed.

She glanced up and saw Mitch and Simon off to the side of the thirty-by-fifty-foot Bible at the top.

❧

Simon left the vehicle and made his way over to the seating area at the top of the hill. There weren't any sightseers that day. Mitch parked the SUV nearby and glanced at Will dozing in his car seat. He rolled down the window in case he woke and walked over to look down the hill. The others looked small in the distance.

"Something else, isn't it?" he commented, glancing back at Simon.

"Yeah."

"Want me to take some photos for you?"

Simon handed him the phone and Mitch snapped pictures of the others climbing toward them.

"You okay, buddy?" he asked when he noticed Simon's sad expression.

"Just thinking about my mom and dad."

Mitch placed a hand on Simon's shoulder. "Good memories, I hope?"

The boy bravely fought back tears. "Why did they have to die like that, Mitch? Who would do something so mean? Mom and Dad never hurt anyone."

Mitch could have told him there was a lot of depravity out there, but Simon was too young for that. "Some things can't be explained."

"I know," he agreed glumly. "If Mom and Dad had gone to church with us that day, they'd still be alive."

Mitch shrugged. "You can't be sure of that, Simon. Your parents didn't deserve to be killed any more than you and Ari deserved to lose them."

Simon sniffed. "And Ari didn't deserve to lose her voice. Do you think she'll ever talk again, Mitch?"

"I do. One day she'll break free of whatever is holding her back and she'll be normal again." He bent to retrieve something shiny in the gravel. Mitch flipped the dime in Simon's direction and the boy caught it. "Until then, she's still the sister you've always known. She loves you. A lot. It's okay to miss your parents, Simon. Okay to talk about them when you're sad. Okay to share your good memories. And your anger for what this person has done to your family."

Simon's brow creased with worry. "I don't want to upset Ari."

Mitch recognized that attitude from when he and Jen lost their parents. He hadn't wanted to upset his sister either. But Jen had been a kid. Ari was an adult. "I'm sure Ari would love to hear what you have to say. Right now she's trapped in a world where she can't voice her pain but she's suffering, too. Could be something you say will make her feel better."

Mitch sat down next to Simon and laid a comforting arm around his shoulders.

"What am I going to do, Mitch?" the boy asked. "Who's going to take care of me?"

"Ari," Mitch said without hesitation. "Are you afraid she doesn't want you? She's been appointed as your guardian."

"But she has a job. Like Daddy."

"Her job won't stand in the way of her taking care of you, Simon. She worries that she might not be a good parent, but I think she'll be the best. Sometimes she might be weird, but you need to remember that she wants to keep you safe when she doesn't allow you do something you really want to do."

"Like fishing?"

"Exactly. Though I think the fishing had more to do with me than you. She didn't know me well enough to trust me when I first offered."

"I think she'll let me go again. I liked fishing yesterday."

Mitch smiled at the boy. He wanted to tell him there would be times when he wanted to talk to his mom or dad about something and it would hurt because they weren't there. That there would be times when a boy needed his dad, and he might not feel comfortable talking to his sister. But Ari would be there to help him through the stages of grief, and they would survive the nightmare of their loss.

Will's screams reverberated throughout the area. Mitch rushed to remove him from the car seat.

"Hey, buddy, take it down a few decibels," he encouraged as he jiggled the baby. He glanced at Simon and said, "Kid's got a powerful set of lungs on him."

Simon nodded, poking his fingers into his ears.

Mitch carried his nephew over to the hilltop and pointed. "There's your mom."

The baby cried harder, and Jen picked up her pace as she neared the halfway point.

He called, "Take your time. He's fine." Mitch carried his nephew over to the seating area. "Look Will, here's your old buddy Simon."

"Hey Will," Simon said, holding his hands over his face and playing a modified peekaboo that occupied the baby's attention for a few minutes. Mitch popped a pacifier into the baby's mouth when he thought he might start to cry again.

The others cleared the top as the sky turned darker and the clouds that had threatened all morning spilled heavy raindrops.

"Looks like this visit may be a rainout," Mitch said, gathering the baby and handing Simon his crutches.

They piled into the SUV, shaking off the water.

"I knew it would rain," Gary mumbled. "Always does when we commune with nature. Do we wait to see if it stops or go back to the house?"

"Let's ride for a few minutes," Jen suggested, playing with Will as she fastened him into his car seat.

Mitch backed the SUV out of the parking space and drove along the unpaved path. They passed a marker.

Paper rattled and Jen said, "That's the One Fold, One Shepherd marker. It's meant to symbolize God's perfect plan for Christian unity. He'll be our Shepherd and we'll be His flock."

Mitch followed the sign when the road split and pointed to the flags. "What's this, Jen?"

"All Nations Cross. The world's largest cross of its kind. We're on All Nations Mountain. The flags represent every nation of the world."

"There's the United States," Simon declared.

Mitch punched his shoulder playfully. "Good job, buddy."

Simon grinned.

Mitch drove until the road dead-ended. "What's this?"

"I'm not sure," Jen said. There were engraved markers and concrete steps.

Mitch turned around and drove back down the hill. The rain seemed determined to linger. He parked at the gift shop. "Anyone need a bathroom break? Something to eat? They have a grill inside."

"Come on, Ari," Jen said. "We'll visit the ladies' room and the gift shop."

The men opted to wait in the car.

There was a duck pond off to the side. "Look Will, ducks," Gary said, trying to divert his son's attention from his missing mother. "Hope she doesn't buy out the place."

Mitch grinned. His sister did like to shop. "Simon and I were talking about some of the other stuff there is to do around here. There's a canopy tour outside Bryson City, but the minimum age is ten."

"I doubt Ari would go along with that anyway," Gary said. "He's already broken his leg. No need to break his neck, too."

"Oh, come on, Gary, they have state-of-the-art equipment on those rides."

"Not for me."

"There's the Great Smoky Mountains Railroad out of Bryson City. And Chimney Rock."

"Seen Chimney Rock and Lake Lure," Gary said. "There's a real curvy road up through the mountains to get you there. Except for that fast ride up in the twenty-six-story elevator, it's pretty much all climbing."

Mitch started to laugh. "Have you noticed everything seems to come back to taking an elevator or walking?"

"Yeah," Gary pronounced glumly.

The women came out of the gift shop, each carrying a small bag.

"Souvenirs," Jen announced as she tucked hers inside her purse. "I think this trip's a bust. Lady inside said the front will probably hang around the rest of the day."

"Home it is," Mitch said.

As they drove through the park, Jen pointed out the replica of Mount Calvary, the baptismal pool, the tomb, and the Bethlehem Star. "That tower is seventy-five feet tall. And that's the Arise, Shine marker. It commemorates the church's fulfillment of the prophecy recorded in Isaiah 60:1. Those are the Psalms of Praise, and that entrance takes you up through Prayer Mountain. That's where the road dead-ends," Jen said. "Three hundred and twenty steps to the top, Gary."

Everyone laughed.

"And no elevator," Jen teased. "Too bad it started to rain. I think I might have wanted you to see that with me."

Gary grinned. "God truly does answer prayers."

The rain fell steadily as they drove along the road leading back to the house.

"Let's ride down to the end of the road and see the Tennessee Valley Authority setup," Gary said.

They parked and looked out over the water with the shadowy mountains in the background.

"Definitely a study in grays," Jen said.

"It's too depressing," Gary said. "Let's go home."

Back at the houses, they said their good-byes and went their separate ways. Mitch helped Simon into the house. "What did we plan for lunch?" he asked.

Ari opened the freezer and glanced at the packages of frozen meat.

"We could drive into Murphy for fast food," Mitch suggested.

She shook her head and took packages of sliced meat and cheese from the fridge and assembled sandwiches. She added dill pickles and potato chips, and they sat at the kitchen island. Before they ate, Ari bowed her head and Simon said grace.

"You make a tasty sandwich," Mitch said after swallowing his first huge bite. "What are we going to do this afternoon?"

"There's a Monopoly game downstairs," Simon said. "We could play."

"Sounds good. What about you, Ari?"

He chuckled when she waved her hands in a "bring it on" gesture.

&

Ari was glad when Nana and Tom returned home safely. Although Ari had been tied up with business when they first arrived home, she now sat with the woman in the living room, listening as she talked about their trip.

"Here's the picture they took of us." Nana handed over a portfolio holding a photo of her with her sister with a picture of Biltmore on the opposite side. "You really need to see this place. It's the largest private residence in America. The guide said George Vanderbilt and his mom visited and he was going to build a small house and then decided to construct something that suited the mountains. It's about as big as a mountain."

The woman chattered on.

"All of it was done without public funds. They even had the first forestry program. With all those rooms, guess they needed it to keep the home fires burning." She chuckled at her own joke.

Ari loved Nana's enthusiasm and the way she shared random facts. She'd obviously enjoyed her time at Biltmore.

How was the spa day?

"I'm not one for all that pampering, but Ellie loved it."

I hope you enjoyed your birthday, Ari wrote.

"I did. Tom took us out to dinner. Ellie is quite taken with him. Told her she's too old for him. What did you do while we were gone?"

Ari wrote about the guys fishing on the lake and how they had visited Fields of the Wood Bible Park.

"We'll have to come back," Nana said. "Everyone says we have to see the mountains in the fall to truly appreciate them."

I have to go to Chicago, Ari wrote on the whiteboard. *Something is happening and I need to sort it out.*

"I'll get our things packed."

She shook her head. *Mitch and Gary are going with me. I need you to stay here with Simon. Jen and Will are going to stay, so I told her to come and stay with you. They can use my room. Tom's going to be over at the other house.*

"If that's what you want."

I'd love to take you and Simon home, Ari wrote, *But we aren't safe there.*

Nana nodded agreement. "Take care of yourself, Ari. Don't take any chances."

I don't plan to.

eleven

Gary made arrangements for the private plane that flew them into O'Hare. From there they took a rental vehicle to the hotel. Gary went for their room keys while Ari waited with Mitch in the vehicle.

"Okay?" he asked, looking back at her from the driver's seat.

She wondered if he realized how often he asked her that. She wasn't okay. This was her hotel. She should be able to walk in the front door with her head held high, not be forced to sneak in through the service elevator.

He reached over the seat and took her hand in his, giving it a gentle squeeze. "We're going to figure out who's behind this."

Ari wished she could voice all her concerns. It would take entirely too long to write down everything that floated around in her head at that particular moment.

Gary returned to the vehicle to escort Ari to the service elevator where Shannon waited. "Mitch needs to run some errands. I'll stay with you while he's gone. Then he can stay with you later while I check in at my office."

Mitch removed his and Ari's suitcases from the trunk. Shannon held the elevator door, and once they were inside, her friend hugged her.

"It's so good to see you. Is Simon okay? How's his leg? I'm sorry," Shannon exclaimed with a little laugh after releasing the barrage of questions. "I've been so worried for you both."

"We're taking good care of them," Gary offered. The elevator stopped on the tenth floor.

Shannon smiled and said, "I know you are. Now, what do we do first?"

"Lunch would be good," Gary said, glancing at Ari, who nodded agreement.

"Let's go to your room, and I'll have the chef send up a meal. The managers are aware you're in the building, but we haven't told the rest of the staff."

Shannon unlocked the door. "If anyone catches on to you being here, we'll tell them you're doing an undercover quality check."

Ari laughed at the woman's grin.

After lunch, she reviewed hotel operations with Shannon and then took a nap. Gary told her he'd be across the hall. Mitch tapped on the door a few hours later to let her know he was back.

That evening he came over to call the house in North Carolina on the speakerphone so Ari could check in and hear how things were going in her absence.

"Jen and I are playing video games," Simon told them. "She's good."

Mitch chuckled. "Watch her, Simon. She cheats."

"I do not," Jen yelled in mock offense.

Ari and Mitch left the hotel early the next day. He looked very handsome in the dark suit. She could tell from the cut and fit of the material that it was expensive. She wondered if that had been his errand. She hoped he hadn't bought a suit for her sake.

They entered the Kent corporate office building via Charles Kent's private elevator and met with her father's assistant, Shirley O'Brien. The woman hugged her and said how sorry she was and how she missed Mr. Kent.

Ari managed to nod and smile sadly at the woman.

"I've placed all the documents you requested on your father's desk. Are you going to be able to work in there?"

Ari would rather have been anywhere else, but she had to do this. Not because her father expected it of her, but rather because she demanded it of herself.

"I'm Mitchell Ellis, Mrs. O'Brien. Either Gary Bishop or myself will be with Ms. Kent here in the office and the boardroom."

She noted the way the woman gave him the once-over and the little nod of approval she offered in return.

"I'll be here at my desk. Let me know if there's anything you need. Anything at all."

"Thank you." Mitch took Ari's arm and walked over to the big carved wooden door to her father's office. He turned the knob and Ari stepped inside. Nowhere else on earth would she find a place where his presence was more obvious. The penthouse was her mother's domain. This office was her father's.

The room smelled of expensive leather and his favorite cologne. The walls reflected his love of art. Ari paused as she touched the large leather chair behind the desk. He'd joked about the chair when it first came in, saying it was more comfortable than any sofa he'd ever sat on. Now it would be her chair.

Moisture filled her eyes and she dabbed carefully at her eyelashes, hoping not to smudge her mascara. She'd probably find out if it held up to the waterproof claim before the day was over.

"You okay?" Mitch asked.

She flashed him a smile and shrugged, drawing in a deep breath before she rolled out the chair and plunked down.

Ari didn't feel much older than when she was a child and waited for her father to complete his work. She leaned forward and pulled the first folder from the pile. She had a lot of material to cover before the board meeting.

She studied the agenda outlining what would be covered.

Other folders contained financial documents, contracts, and plans for future expansion. Ari feared she'd never finish in time.

Mitch sat on the sofa by the door, first reading the paper he'd brought along and then a paperback. They followed the same format on Wednesday.

Thursday morning at eight, the phone buzzed. When Ari answered, Mrs. O'Brien informed her that Erik George of Kearns, George, and Howe had arrived for their meeting.

Mitch stood and opened the door, gesturing the man inside. Erik George nodded at him before advancing in her direction, his hand outstretched. "Ari, so good to have you back in Chicago. Hope you're doing well?"

She smiled graciously and indicated the chair on the opposite side of the desk.

"Thank you for the update on Todd Langan's activity. We had no idea he has been harassing you. I apologize."

Ari glanced at Mitch. They had debated whether the firm's partners had any idea of Todd's efforts on their behalf.

"I regret the situation that has brought us together but assure you it's a temporary setback at best. Understandable given your experience. No reason the company can't continue to operate."

She reached for the whiteboard and wrote, *"Todd Langan seems extremely eager to have my parents' will read. Do you know why?"*

"Todd can be overzealous at times. Perhaps he felt he needed the information to advise you properly. Whatever the case, I have a copy of the will here and plan to make you aware of the facts before the meeting."

He reached for his briefcase and Mitch moved closer to Ari, ready to offer the support she might need.

Erik George set the case on the other visitor chair and pulled out the legal document. Flipping the first page, he said, "Other than a few minor bequests, your parents left the majority of their estate to you."

Stunned, Ari touched her chest.

He nodded. "After Simon was born, your father asked me to draw up papers giving your mother control of 51 percent of their company shares. They own 60 percent of the company shares. At the time I assumed it had to do with Michelle giving him a son. Later, when the wills were drafted, your mother left her shares to you. Your father split his shares equally between you and Simon. They also designated you as Simon's legal guardian in the event something happened to them. I assume you're willing to assume that responsibility?"

"Without doubt," she wrote in dark print, two exclamation points at the end.

He nodded. "You control your parents' shares plus the additional shares you were given when you joined the firm."

Ari didn't understand her mother's blatant show of favoritism. Why had they not inherited equally? Did it have something to do with Simon being a minor? Was there another stipulation regarding his coming of age? Still, that didn't mean he wasn't entitled to a fair division of the shares.

"I must also tell you that your mother stipulated that the 51 percent go to charity if you challenge the will. She does say that she feels you are more than capable of carrying on their legacy and believes you will do what is best for Kent Enterprises."

She looked at Mitch.

Erik George continued, "There are a few more items we need to cover before we go to the boardroom today. I have no doubt you'll be appointed CEO. I also plan to apprise Todd and the board that he no longer serves as counsel for the firm."

"Security?" Mitch requested.

"I doubt Todd will cause trouble. While he may not be

happy, he should leave the room without causing a scene."

Mitch glanced at Ari and she nodded.

"Don't say anything until he reveals his plan."

"Pardon?" Erik looked taken aback by his comment.

Mitch glanced at Ari and back at the lawyer. "We need to know Langan's intent. We suspect he's behind this plan. Who has been proposed to take on the role of CEO until Ari is deemed competent?"

Erik looked uncomfortable. "Ann Radnor."

"Langan's fiancée? What qualifies her?" Mitch asked.

"I learned what I know from talking to the board members who support Ari. This woman has no experience beyond the brief time she worked as Charles Kent's assistant several years ago. A fact that has made these board members question Todd's intent." The lawyer glanced at his watch. "I suggest we run over the agenda and put together a plan of attack."

The three of them sat talking, Ari writing notes on the whiteboard.

The attorney gave a quick overview of the plan. "Is that correct?"

Ari nodded.

Erik George pushed up the french cuff of his shirt and looked at his watch. "It's almost ten. Are we ready for the boardroom?"

Ari retreated to her father's executive washroom. She emerged a few minutes later, her hair twisted into a neat chignon at the base of her neck and her makeup and lipstick refreshed. She slipped her arms into the sleeves of the black silk suit coat Mitch held and smoothed it into place. The high heels pushed her up to his shoulder height.

"Ready?" he asked.

She drew in a deep breath and nodded.

Mitch gave her arm a gentle squeeze and led the way

through the double doors. Ari strode into the room and took a seat at the head of the table. Mitch went to stand behind her next to Gary, who had opted to meet them in the boardroom.

Ari focused on Todd Langan. While he appeared pleased to see her present, she noted the suspicion in his eyes. Had he expected that he could carry off this upheaval and leave her in the dark? At least Todd would realize she was as much in the know away from her company as in the office.

The meeting began. She noted that Ann Radnor was not in the boardroom. The underlying anger she felt toward the two of them gave her the impetus she needed to attack the situation. They would not take her company away from her.

Ari brushed moist hands along the expensive suit skirt and lifted her hands to the laptop keyboard. A projector displayed the computer screen on the far wall.

I APOLOGIZE FOR THIS UNUSUAL FORM OF COMMUNI-
CATION, BUT AS MOST OF YOU ARE AWARE, I AM UNABLE
TO SPEAK. I HAVE BEEN DIAGNOSED AS SUFFERING FROM
CONVERSION DISORDER. MY DOCTOR, DWAYNE GRAVES,
IS PRESENT AND WILL ANSWER ANY QUESTIONS YOU MAY
HAVE.

The board members listened avidly as the doctor outlined the specifics of her condition. "I assure you Ms. Kent is 100 percent capable of carrying on with her duties. Her ability to speak could return as quickly as it left. The shock of finding. . . Well, we can imagine how traumatizing the experience was for her."

Cedric Reynolds spoke up. "I'm sorry for all she's been through, but I'm concerned about how her problems will affect the company."

Ari eyed him and began to type furiously.

No one here has more to lose than Simon and myself. While I understand your concerns, I assure you my condition does not stand in the way of doing my job. You've seen the figures on the Hotel Kent Chicago. My team increased the profits there by nearly 25 percent in three years. I can assure you my goal is to do the same for the entire Kent organization.

And if, for whatever reason, I find I cannot perform my duties, I'll be the first to recommend hiring a CEO.

She sounded like a pageant winner, Ari thought as the words appeared on the screen.

"How can a mute conduct business?"

All heads swiveled in Todd's direction. Several people appeared shocked by his outburst.

Erik George stood from his place in the back of the room. "I don't believe Ms. Kent's ability to perform her job is in question, Todd. Everyone here is aware of Ari's history with the company. She possesses an MBA from a prestigious university, and she trained with her father to step into the role."

"Sir, I didn't mean to imply—"

Erik George continued, "After speaking with Ms. Kent this morning, I can assure you she is in no way deficient in her ability to perform her duties. And as I have informed her today, she is the beneficiary of the majority of her parents' shares, and as young Simon's guardian, she controls his shares as well. She also has the shares she was given when she joined the company."

"She can't talk. How does she expect to represent the company?" Reynolds asked.

Ari looked from him to Todd. Here were her

troublemakers. If she remembered correctly, Reynolds's small number of shares had come to him via an elderly aunt.

"Ms. Kent can hear, and if you'll address your concerns to her, I'm sure she'll respond," Mitch ground out. "She was, and still is, in fear for her life. Coming here today could very well put her in jeopardy."

Ari stared at Mitch. What had set him off?

"You're all so worried about your bank accounts that you can't find a bit of sympathy in your hearts for two innocents robbed of their parents. I hope none of you ever have to confront the same devil Ari's living with right now."

Angry, quiet mumbling started among the board.

"How dare you," Cedric Reynolds said, rising to his feet. "What gives you the right to judge our actions?"

Mitch stood tall and spoke confidently. "I can tell you without reservation that Arianna Kent's inability to speak has nothing to do with her ability to run this organization. And if this board takes action because of her condition, it will be a blatant case of discrimination."

"Get out," Reynolds ordered, pointing to the door.

"Gentlemen," Dwayne Graves called, "Dr. Ellis is as upset by what he's witnessed here today as I am. Despite any misgivings you may have, Ms. Kent's inability to speak in no way compromises her competency to operate her parents' company."

Ari looked from one man to the other. Dr. Ellis? No. This was Mitchell Ellis. He worked for Bishop Security.

Voices raised as each member tried to outtalk the other.

Finally, Erik George called out, "Ladies. Gentlemen. Please. Let's keep this to the business at hand. Out of fairness to the Kent family, my recommendation is that you give Ms. Kent time to prepare a plan showing how she proposes to conduct business until such a time as her voice returns.

"And effective immediately, Todd Langan will no longer

serve as counsel for Kent Enterprises. Per Ms. Kent's request, I have assumed the role as of today."

As Erik had predicted, Todd charged from the room. Stunned by the revelations of the boardroom, Ari texted Gary to get her out of there. He stepped forward to escort her. She refused to look at Mitch as she walked past.

❧

Mitch tried to push past the press of board members leaving the room. It was the voice that caught his attention. A voice he'd heard weekly for years now. He looked for and found the woman.

A tall, dark-haired woman clung to Ari's arm. Gary stepped forward to remove her hand and blocked Mitch's view.

"Where is Simon? How is he?" the woman demanded almost frantically.

Ari pulled herself free.

"Please, Ari. Listen to me," she pleaded. "I can help you. I know how your father did business. Right now you're upset with me and with Todd, but we want to help."

Ari walked away and the woman called, "You forced us to do this. You wouldn't return Todd's calls. He had to do what was best for the company. For Simon."

The crowd cleared and Mitch looked straight into the woman's eyes. "Raquel? What are you doing here?" he demanded.

She lowered her head slightly, averting her gaze. "My name is Ann Radnor."

Who was she trying to fool? He'd know her anywhere. This woman was Raquel Wilson.

twelve

"I want you to take me back to Simon."

Mitch read the message Ari had written to Gary on the whiteboard and knew he'd messed up big-time. He should have told her the truth before going into the boardroom.

"You'll have to return to Murphy with Mitch or wait until I can take you," Gary told her. "Something has come up and I can't leave now. He has your best interests at heart, Ari. You can't deny that he performed his duties admirably."

She didn't write a reply to that. The chilling blast of anger in her green gaze spoke of her feelings of betrayal.

"I'll go alone."

"No, you won't," Mitch declared. "You're safe with me. Once we arrive back in Murphy, I'll stay until Gary sends a replacement. Then I'll get out of your life forever."

Ari burst into tears and ran into the bathroom. Mitch felt like a total jerk.

Later that day, they traveled to O'Hare in a helicopter to avoid the crush of media that had hounded her ever since learning of her presence at the board meeting. Settling in the luxurious private plane, they waited while the crew performed their flight check.

"Please let me explain," Mitch pleaded.

Ari turned to stare out the window.

She wouldn't listen. Hadn't listened to a word he'd said since his explosion in the boardroom. He'd known the truth would come out. And he couldn't talk his way around what he had done.

"This is why I didn't tell you. I knew how you'd react. You

124

think I'm here in the capacity of psychiatrist, but I'm not. I wanted to protect you and Simon."

Thin lines creased between her brows.

"When Gary asked to use the houses. . ."

Her head jerked up to look at him.

"Yes, the houses belong to me," he admitted. "I frequently visit the mountains and was scheduled for a three-week vacation when I volunteered to help. When Dwayne told me what happened, I was overcome by this need to help you and Simon to feel safe. I had to help.

"I did help," Mitch declared. "I lost sleep to take care of you in every way I could. I've been your friend. I can't deny that your condition interests me because I want you to recover."

Ari stood and took a seat as far away from him as possible. The rest of the journey passed in silence. As they neared the mountains, lightning flashes in the dark night indicated a storm. Mitch noted the way she closed the window shade and then her eyes as it came nearer.

At the airport, they deplaned in a downpour. Ari waited in the car as Mitch collected their luggage. His clothes were soaked when he climbed into the driver's seat.

The heavy rain made the trip even longer. Sharp jagged slashes of lightning and booming peals of thunder surrounded them, and Ari withdrew even deeper within herself. Mitch had to pull over a couple of times when visibility got so bad he couldn't see to drive.

He made a few more aborted attempts to explain before giving up. She wasn't willing to listen. In her eyes, he was no better than Langan and Radnor. A Judas who had infiltrated her home and pretended to care about her.

It wasn't a pretense. He did care for her. A great deal.

"I never intended to hurt you," he said as he turned into the Bear Paw entrance and rolled to a stop at the guardhouse.

"Welcome back," the security guard said.

They both glanced up when a nearby lightning strike seemed a bit too close for comfort.

"Thanks. Nasty weather."

"Definitely," the man agreed. "Take care going to the houses. There have been reports of washouts from a couple of homeowners."

"We'll keep our eyes open."

Mitch powered up the window and drove forward. "Please understand, Ari. It was never my intention to keep this from you indefinitely. You had enough going on in your life. You didn't need more to worry about then or now. You have a major task ahead of you in the next month. Let me help."

Mitch turned onto their road. Silence reigned. He glanced over at her. "Please. . ."

Before he could continue, the vehicle tipped off the side of the mountain.

"Ari! Hold on!" he yelled as they slid sideways, banging against tree after tree like a pinball machine until one tree refused to let them pass. Mitch's head hit the window with a sickening thud, causing the glass to spiderweb. He groaned as the side air bag covered him. Blackness filled his world and he knew no more.

☙

Blood spilled from Mitch's head. Too much blood. Ari closed her eyes against the horrible image, fighting back waves of nausea and encroaching darkness.

She drew in several deep breaths. She had to get help. Terror spurred her into action. Ari searched for an out. The window. She tried the control. It wouldn't work. A tool. She needed something to break the glass.

Then she could climb out and go for help. She pulled open the glove compartment, her hand closing around a flashlight. The metal tube would serve her purpose, Ari thought as she attempted to maneuver herself around to strike the glass.

The pressure of the seat belt cut into her as she hung from the passenger side of the vehicle. If she released the latch, she'd tumble onto Mitch and cause him even greater injury.

As she raised the flashlight, the communication service in the vehicle came to life. "Mr. Ellis, we have a report this vehicle has been involved in an accident. Are you okay?" the representative called.

Answer her, Mitch, Ari willed silently. *She's asking you a question.* He didn't stir. Ari didn't know how many minutes had passed without his regaining consciousness.

No, he definitely wasn't okay. Mitch was in trouble. She had to do something. She had to help him. Now. Ari opened her mouth, so afraid she'd fail this man who meant so much to them.

"Please," she began, her voice quavering and unfamiliar after so long. She gained volume as she said, "Mr. Ellis is badly injured. We slipped off the side of the mountain. A tree is all that's keeping us from tumbling farther."

"Can you verify the address of where you are?"

She knew the name of the neighborhood but not the street. Ari fumbled around in her coat pocket and pulled out her phone, thankful she hadn't put it in her purse. "Hold on." She dialed the house and demanded, "What's the address here?"

"Ari? Is that you?" Nana demanded suspiciously.

"Nana, yes. I need the address. Mitch is injured. I'm trying to get help."

Tom came on the line and gave her their location. "I'm coming down."

She recited the address to the woman at the communications center.

"We'll notify the police."

"Ari?" Tom called on the phone. "Are you hurt?"

"No, but Mitch slammed his head against the window. There's lots of blood."

"Did the window break?"

"No. It cracked. He's been unconscious for several minutes."

"I'm coming. Hang on. We'll get help."

She knew he didn't mean the "hang on" part literally, but that was exactly what she was doing. "Please be all right," she prayed as she looked down on Mitch's still form. Minutes seemed like hours as they passed with no immediate sign of help.

Finally, a raincoat-clad Tom and Jen ran toward the vehicle, their flashlights bobbing in the darkness. Rain sluiced down the front window, distorting Ari's vision.

Tom grabbed the door handle. He banged on the side and shouted for her to unlock the door. Ari fumbled around and tried to grab the knob but couldn't get her fingers around the rounded top. It was too low in the opening. She pushed the shoulder harness down and left the seat belt in place.

The first movement rocked the vehicle slightly. She tried again without as much momentum. It took several tries to reach the remote hanging from the ignition, but she finally managed to grab hold and push the button for the door lock.

Tom pulled the door up. Jen grabbed and held on so that it wouldn't slam back on Ari.

"Can you shove your legs over the side?"

"No," Ari said. "If I release the seat belt, I'll fall on Mitch."

"Give me your hand," Tom said. "I'll hold you when you release the latch."

"It won't work."

Siren wails could be heard in the distance.

Tom pulled himself up on the side of the vehicle and called to Mitch. No response. The vehicle shifted slightly.

"Be careful," Ari warned. "That tree is all that's keeping us from falling."

The ambulance pulled up, keeping its distance from the gaping asphalt above them. The attendants came running only to realize they couldn't do anything until the vehicle was moved. The wrecker and police officer arrived at the same time.

The wrecker driver took several precious minutes to connect the cables, and then with a slow movement, the vehicle came back onto the road. Tom helped Ari from the vehicle. She stood on wobbly legs, very aware of how frightened she'd been.

"Are you okay?" Jen asked, supporting Ari with an arm around her waist.

"I'm fine."

Her gaze turned to the other side of the vehicle, where the ambulance attendants used equipment to force open the jammed door. They checked Mitch's vitals, supported his neck with a brace, and carefully transferred him to the stretcher. Once loaded with the patient, the vehicle reversed down the street and Ari nearly collapsed from exhaustion.

Jen pointed to the hole and asked, "How are we going to get past that to get to the hospital?"

"I'll take you," the officer said.

"Thank you. I'm Jennifer Bishop, Mitch Ellis's sister. This is Arianna Kent. She needs to be checked as well. She was in the vehicle with my brother."

Ari shook her head, indicating she was fine.

"Relax," Jen instructed, her arm around Ari's shoulders as she hugged her close.

Ari found this to be an impossible task. She was soaking wet. The officer cranked up the heat. She couldn't be still and fidgeted nervously in the backseat of the police car. How could she have treated Mitch like that? Was he okay?

The officer took them to the Murphy Medical Center. Jen led her inside and one of the nurses brought a warm blanket.

Ari wrapped it tightly about herself, welcoming the comfort. She shivered uncontrollably.

"Drink this," Jen said, handing her a cup of hot coffee.

Ari warmed her hands slightly before taking a gulp.

"Careful," Jen warned, too late as Ari felt the stinging burn to her tongue.

"The doctor is with Mr. Ellis in the examining room," the nurse told them.

"Thank you." After the woman left, Jen turned to Ari. "When did you get your voice back?"

"When that communication service representative asked Mitch if he was okay, I knew I had to get help for him. I was so afraid."

"He's going to be fine, Ari."

She looked into Jen's eyes and saw hope. Here she was being comforted when this woman needed comfort. Her brother lay battered and bleeding in the exam room.

"I'm sorry, Jen. I'm so selfish."

A smile touched her face. "It's not your fault the road caved in."

"It's my fault he wasn't paying attention," Ari offered sadly. "We had a fight. Mitch didn't tell me he was a psychiatrist. He knew I believed he worked security for Gary. He said he wanted to protect us."

"Then that was his intent. Mitch isn't the type to play games, Ari. When Gary asked to use the houses, he told him he was scheduled for a vacation. Gary was surprised when Mitch offered to help out, but he was also concerned about sending you to North Carolina with people he didn't know."

"Then why?"

"Mitch has his reasons. He always does."

Ari mulled that over as they waited. What reason could he possibly have had? He hadn't known them. Hadn't known their parents. Why would he give up his vacation to work security?

The ER doctor came to talk with them. "Mrs. Bishop, I'm Doctor Stokes. Mr. Ellis has a two-inch laceration at his hairline which we will staple closed. He hasn't regained consciousness yet. So we're running tests and monitoring his brain activity."

Ari looked at the man through a haze. Mitch had to be all right. She could see his face, his beautiful face, and couldn't help but feel it was all her fault. If he hadn't been trying to convince her of his innocence, he would have paid more attention to his driving. Ari felt herself falling.

Ari's eyes fluttered open. She lay on a stretcher with the doctor looking down at her. "What happened?"

"You fainted. How do you feel?" the doctor asked.

"I'm okay."

"Rest for a while," he said, pulling a sheet over Ari's body. "We'll see how you feel and decide if you should be admitted."

He looked at Jen. "Stay with her. I'll let you know as soon as I have more information about your brother."

The doctor left, and Jen pulled a chair over next to the bed. She reached for Ari's hand and soothed her with the same gentle murmuring she used with Will. "It's going to be okay," she whispered. "Mitch will be fine. I know he will."

"Pray for him," Ari said.

"Yes," Jen agreed. "Let's pray now."

They bowed their heads and Jen said, "Blessed Father, we come to You seeking Your protection for our loved one. You know what's going on with Mitch right now and we pray that You heal him with Your powerful touch. Touch his heart and remind him that he's still Your child."

"Is Mitch a believer?" Ari asked softly.

"Our parents took us to church when we were kids. He accepted Christ when he was eleven. Then our parents died and he stopped going to church.

"Aunt Sandy said he needed time. It was pretty bad. He was burned trying to rescue Mom and Dad. The investigator said they had already been overcome by smoke when he went in. He nearly died."

"I've seen his scars," she said softly. "They looked so painful."

"It was bad, but he survived."

Mitch understood loss. He had been so young. Only thirteen.

"What happened?"

"Old house. Faulty wiring. Their bedroom was on the opposite end of the house from ours. Mitch got me outside before going back in for our parents."

"Didn't anyone try to stop him?"

"It was in the wee hours of the morning. The house was fully engulfed by the time the fire department arrived. Two neighbors rescued Mitch. He hadn't made it beyond the living room when the smoke fumes overcame him. I feared he would die then.

"But he recovered and we went to live with Aunt Sandy. She's our mom's sister. Never married. Taking on two adolescents couldn't have been easy for her, but she didn't hesitate. You're like her. Simon's blessed to have you."

"I hope I'm up to the task."

"Love is all Simon needs. Give him that and the rest will come naturally. Not to say you won't experience some rocky paths along the way, but love will make it right for you both in the end."

"Why didn't Mitch tell me about what happened to him?"

Jen shrugged. "He doesn't talk about it often. He's a good man, Ari. Mitch used his pain and suffering to help others overcome theirs. He's good at listening and asking the right questions. It's his gift. Now, you should rest."

Ari closed her eyes. Why had Mitch never spoken of his

parents' deaths? Maybe it had been too soon. They'd known each other for such a short time.

Still, he'd hurt her with his secret identity. Hearing Dwayne Graves call him Dr. Ellis had come as a great shock on top of so many others. It had been more than she could handle. She wanted to trust him with all her heart but didn't know how she could.

&

"Ari," Mitch called, holding out his hand to her. He couldn't disguise his joy at seeing her. It was her first visit since he'd awakened. He'd been so afraid she wouldn't come. She looked so good he wanted to hug her.

She kept her distance, and the hospital bed seemed more like a prison than a place of healing. His head hurt, the lump beneath the white bandage tender and large.

His sister had told him how Ari had spoken to summon help for him.

"Jen says the doctor says you're doing better," Ari said.

He sucked in a breath at the low, honeyed sound. Exactly as he'd imagined all those times when he'd longed to hear her speak. Soft-spoken and delightful, as pleasing as he'd dreamed it would be. Their time without a spoken word seemed so long ago. He longed to hear more.

"Your voice," Mitch said. "Jen told me. You sound exactly as I thought you would."

She seemed uncomfortable with his comments.

"I'm glad to have my voice back," Ari said finally, maintaining her distance.

"Please, Ari," he beseeched, trying to sit up in the bed. "I know you're angry. You have a right to be. I don't have any excuse. I do know Dwayne and we talked, but at no point did he ask me to do a consultation. In fact, when I offered, he said you would refuse.

"I didn't take the security job to check you out. Though I

have to admit I was curious. I am a doctor after all. And you have to admit your situation merited consideration.

"But as I told you, the houses belong to me. I knew the area. I worked security back when I was in college. I honestly wanted to protect you and Simon. I wanted you to have the time you needed to recuperate."

"Maybe it goes back to losing your parents?" she suggested. "Jen told me what happened. Why didn't you ever tell me about them? I thought we were friends."

"We were—we are. I didn't want to add to your grief. You were already struggling with what had happened to you. I didn't want you feeling sorry for me about something that happened so many years ago."

"Knowing you'd been there and understood would have been reassuring. The loss of your parents was as tragic and senseless as that of my parents."

"I failed, Ari. I let them die in that fire."

"Not your fault," she said with a shake of her head. "It was one of those terrible things that happen and we can't explain why."

"It's been a driving force in my life. I've been told my need to help others stems from that night."

"Probably," she answered him thickly. Her lashes dropped to hide her hurt. "I trusted you, Mitch. Told you things I never told anyone else. Do you understand why I feel betrayed?"

Mitch nodded. He stopped and grimaced with the pain. One glimpse of her hurt expression and he felt worse than Judas.

"I won't tell your secrets. I'm a doctor. I deal with patient confidentiality all the time."

Frustrated by his comment, she uttered, "I am not your patient. Don't you understand? I never wanted to be your patient."

"You weren't," he insisted. "We're friends. More than friends. I care about you and Simon. My initial decision may have been made out of sympathy, but I did what I needed to do to keep you safe."

Ari didn't understand. "Why?"

Her entire being seemed filled with waiting. What did she want to hear from him?

"Because I had to," Mitch admitted. "I felt the attraction the moment I laid eyes on you, and it's strengthened as we've gotten to know each other better. I want your parents' killers found so you can put this behind you."

She struggled to speak. Mitch knew the misery of that night remained with her.

"I can't put it behind me. It's there, haunting me every step of the way. Making me question why God would let something like this happen."

"You can," Mitch insisted, resting his throbbing head against the pillows as he spoke. "In time, the pain will fade. Your grief has been so much worse because you couldn't share your feelings.

"Now you can talk it out with Simon and Nana. You can't change what happened. Finding out who did this is not going to bring them back. In fact, the discovery will more than likely provide you with someone to hate. And I know that's something you don't want to do.

"I questioned God, too," Mitch admitted. "My parents were God-fearing Christians. We were in church every time the doors opened. To have them burn to death didn't make sense."

"Do you go to church, Mitch?"

"Now and then. Usually Christmas and Easter with the family."

"Do you believe?"

Do I? The conscious decisions he'd made over the years

not to serve the Lord or attend church had nothing to do with his belief that Jesus Christ died for his sins. "Yes. In all the years since their death, I've kept myself too busy to spare time for God, but I do believe. Now I've witnessed your love for Him and accepted the only person I'm hurting is me. Instead of reaching out and accepting the love He offered, I pushed Him away and pretended it didn't matter.

"You exude a peace that I know comes from your faith. That's why I believe you'll get past this anger at me."

"I've been praying," she admitted.

"Maybe in time," Mitch said softly. "Once life gets back to normal, you'll be busy taking care of Simon and dealing with your work as CEO of Kent Enterprises. I know you'll do a great job. And now that you have your voice back, I doubt the board will be as anxious. Look out for Langan. He's behind that effort in the boardroom. And that woman, the one you call Ann. Watch her as well."

"But he's been removed from the position. There's no reason for him to contact the board."

Suspicions of what Langan might try tugged at Mitch's consciousness. He knew it had something to do with Raquel Wilson, aka Ann Radnor. And unless he was way off base, Charles Kent.

"Watch out for them, Ari."

She nodded. "I will."

"And hopefully you'll find it in your heart to forgive me. I'm going to be praying, too. I live in Chicago. My practice is on the lower floor of my house. Maybe one day we can get together for lunch to discuss this situation?"

She stared at him, and Mitch wished he knew what she was thinking. For so long he'd longed to hear her speak. He wanted to hear more. His injury was so worth the outcome.

"Thanks for all you've done for us, Mitch," she said with a frightening finality. She took a step forward and leaned to kiss his cheek. "I'll pray for your swift recovery. Good-bye."

"Not good-bye," he whispered as she walked out the door. Not as long as he had breath in him to convince her differently.

Mitch spent the intervening hours thinking of Ari. The pain of his head was nothing compared to that of his heart.

"I couldn't stop her," Gary told Mitch when he called a few hours later. "After you talked, she went back to the house, packed up the family, and requested transport back to Chicago. I'm here at the townhouse with her now."

Mitch's heavy sigh made his head hurt worse. "Is she okay? Still talking?"

"Not a lot, but she is talking. Mostly planning how she's going to handle things now that she's back at home. Funny how she broke loose like that to save your sorry self."

Mitch wished Gary's insinuation were true. He'd love nothing more than having Ari right here next to him, soothing his brow and encouraging him to come home soon. "More likely terror galvanized her into action. We were hanging off the side of a mountain with one lone tree keeping us from possibly rolling to our deaths."

"Maybe the tumble was worth it," Gary suggested.

Despite the pounding headache, Mitch decided Gary was right.

"Jen had me bring Will back to Chicago. She's staying there with you until you're released."

Mitch smiled at his little sister's penchant for organizing everyone's life. "I'll send her home. I'm coming back to Chicago as soon as they release me."

"Any word on when that will be?"

"Another day or two. Look after Ari, Gary. She's vulnerable and she's going to be called upon to make decisions she might not be ready to make."

"Ari says she's done with hiding."

"Did she terminate your contract?" Mitch demanded, suddenly fearful that she'd separated herself from Bishop Security because of him.

"No. I've got four men assigned. And Tom's sticking to her like glue."

"I wish we knew the motivation behind the killings."

"Yeah, it would have been nice if they had left a signed confession providing us with all the specifics."

"You know what I mean."

"I know Arianna Kent is a beautiful young woman who will come across more than her fair share of people willing to relieve her of her money. She will develop her scam antennae very quickly."

Mitch suspected his actions had aided in that development. Her reaction to the things he'd been privy to as her friend troubled him. It probably bothered her that he'd been present at the reading of the will. And the other things she'd shared in the comfort of their late-night confidences, such as her concerns over becoming Simon's guardian and taking over the company.

Mitch would never tell anyone what she'd said. It was between the two of them, and that's where it would stay.

"If you talk to Jen before I do, tell her to come see me. I'll talk her into going home."

"I don't think you'll be successful. It's okay, Mitch. After that lick on your head, you probably need a traveling companion. Aunt Sandy will help look after Will."

"He'll miss his mom."

"So hurry up and get out of there and come home."

"The plan is to spend the least possible amount of time in this place. With any luck they'll throw me out soon."

"Getting thrown out is not an option," Gary commented. "You need to stay as long as they feel is necessary. And don't worry about Ari. I plan to be with her every step of the way. She trusts very few people right now, and that's a good thing. She's making plans for her move to the corporate offices. Shannon Crown will take over as GM at the hotel."

He frowned. Ari loved her hotel.

"She's definitely got a huge load resting on those tiny shoulders, but we have to give her credit for taking it on," Gary said. "She wants me to set up a safe area for Simon. She plans to move the occupant out of the office next to hers, remove the existing door, and install a door into her office. She's already got carpenters working on that. I suspect she'll look into hiring a tutor once school starts back."

"What about Dora?"

"Ari is sending her to visit family. She plans to personally vet my man before allowing him to accompany Dora. She's paying for him to stay until they find the killer."

"I'm surprised Dora agreed."

"She won't go without argument. I think Ari considered sending Simon with her but decided it was too much on the woman."

"Probably needs to keep him near anyway," Mitch said. "They have lots to discuss now that Ari has her voice back. They can support and reassure each other through all this."

"I have to run. I'm sure you'll see Jen soon."

"Thanks, Gary."

Half an hour later Jen breezed into his hospital room. She kissed his cheek and placed his shaving kit on the table. "I brought clean pajamas and a robe," she said. "And your slippers. How are you feeling? Head still hurting?"

"I want you to go home. Will needs you more than I do."

Jen sniffed. "Will doesn't have a major gash on his head or a concussion. You need to let me take care of you. Gary can handle our son."

Mitch smiled at his sister. She loved opportunities to tell her older brother what was best for him.

"I need a favor," he said. "Some highly confidential research."

That got her attention. "What kind?"

"The kind you'll need to do in Chicago. You can't tell anyone, but I suspect Michelle Kent isn't Simon's birth mother."

She frowned. "Ari says he's her brother."

"There's something weird about the situation." He shared how Simon had come into Ari's life.

"She came home for spring break and learned she had a brother?" Jen asked.

He nodded slowly, afraid any movement would set off the pounding headache that had begun to ease.

"Tom said Michelle Kent went away in early December and returned home with Simon in early March."

Jen shrugged. "Maybe she went someplace less stressful for the birth."

"But why leave her entire inheritance to Ari? If you had two children, would you favor one over the other? She even stipulated the money would go to charity if Ari tried to change the will. Charles Kent split his equitably."

His sister's expression changed with her sudden curiosity. "That is strange. I can see Ari acting as Simon's guardian and looking out for his interests, but you'd think his mother would have left him equal shares."

"So will you nose around and see what you can find? And keep it to yourself?"

"How will Ari feel if she finds out what we're doing?"

Mitch rubbed his neck. "She's already upset with me, but my gut says there's something going on. I feel as though I'm assembling a puzzle with missing pieces."

"So maybe you have more names you'd like me to research? Confidentially, that is."

He considered this. "Will you tell Gary?"

"He's my husband," she reminded.

"And you should never keep secrets that could harm your relationship. I promise to ask for help when I reach a point where I can't do anything else on my own."

"You're okay with me sharing your Michelle Kent theory?"

Mitch nodded. "So long as he keeps it to himself."

thirteen

Another week passed before Mitch returned to Chicago. After his hospital release, he made arrangements for another place to stay while he contacted companies to repair the damaged roadway.

"Your patients are getting restless," his service told him when he called to let them know he needed a few more days.

"Tell them I was in an accident."

"Raquel Wilson has called several times since you were last in Chicago. Said she must see you right away."

Mitch had a good idea the woman intended to conduct her own fact-finding mission. No doubt she wanted to know about his association with the Kents. "Share what I told you, and if she calls again let her know I'll contact her when I return."

He really wanted to know more about the Ann Radnor persona. Most people who used aliases were up to no good. Was that the case with Ann?

Per doctor's orders, Mitch spent a good portion of each day resting, which for him meant thinking. Today he'd rented the pontoon boat for a fishing trip. As he fished, he thought of Simon's enjoyment of his first time and wished he and Ari were here with him now.

He thought of Ari and Simon often, wondering about their lives in Chicago. Mitch knew from conversations with Gary that they were being careful. He hoped they were happy.

The beautiful summer day was meant for communing with nature. There wasn't a cloud in the sky, and he hadn't seen anyone else on the lake. His phone rang.

"Hey, big brother, whatcha doing?"

Jennifer. He should have known. She had checked on him several times a day since his release from the hospital. "I'm out on Lake Hiwassee, thinking about all the fish you scared away when the phone rang."

She laughed. "Ah, too bad for you but good for the fish."

"Yeah, they're safe for another day. What's up?"

"Thought I'd check in with the results of my research."

"Is it what I thought? Wait, we'd better not discuss this on my cell. Can you call me on a landline in a couple of hours?"

"Sure. I'm on my way to Aunt Sandy's to pick up Will."

"Tell her hello and give him a kiss for me."

"Will do. Talk soon."

Mitch quickly reeled in his line and prepared to head home. Back at the house, he answered the phone on the first ring a couple of hours later. "So what did you find out?"

"I checked the will and verified Michelle Kent left everything to Ari," she said. "That includes the penthouse, which was in Michelle's name, and all her jewelry, which is substantial. Plus she has a large investment portfolio that originated from her parents. The Kents did not have joint accounts. If Ari is her only child, it stands to reason that she would be her sole beneficiary. But how did Simon enter the picture?"

"You didn't find anything?"

"His birth certificate lists the Kents as his parents. If he's adopted, it could have been a private adoption."

"Where does the birth certificate say he was born?"

He could hear the click of computer keys. "Chicago."

"But Michelle Kent wasn't in Chicago when he was born. Jen, what if Charles Kent is his real father?"

"Are you thinking Charles Kent had an affair?"

"Erik George told Ari her father insisted on the stock

division in her mother's favor after Simon was born. There had to be a reason he would do that."

"It's possible the birth mother signed over her rights to him. Mitch, what do you know about this?"

He could almost hear her mind working.

"Ari doesn't doubt that he's her brother."

"He could be her adopted brother. Or her half brother."

"If this has something to do with what happened to the Kents, you should go to the police."

"That's the problem. I'm speculating. Besides, I'm sure they've already checked out everything I've come up with. Not to mention, my theory involves a patient. I could be sued."

Jen grunted and said, "There's no way Charles Kent ever planned to leave his wife. Not after giving her controlling interest. I agree that it must have been a good faith gesture."

"Should we continue to look?"

"Oh definitely. I checked the newspaper archives for anything around the time Simon was born. Michelle Kent went missing from the social register sometime around early December and returned to Chicago in early March with a birth announcement."

That matched what Ari had shared. "You have time to add another name to your list?"

"Sure. Let me have it."

"Todd Langan."

"What am I searching for?"

"Anything on his association with the Kents and Ann Radnor."

"What do I tell Gary?"

"That your brother is the curious sort."

She laughed at the tongue-in-cheek reply. "He already knows that about you."

"Send me a bill for your time."

"This one's on the house."

"Thanks, Jen. I'm flying out tomorrow. Should be home midafternoon."

"How's your head?"

"Still aches now and again. Otherwise I'm fine."

"Well, take care and see you soon. Love you."

"Love you, too."

Mitch pondered what Jen had told him.

Ari and Simon had been in his thoughts all afternoon. Once he returned to Chicago, he planned to double his efforts to gain Ari's forgiveness.

Deciding there was no need to wait, he dialed the number she'd given him. Busy. He looked at the other contacts. Simon's number was right underneath. Mitch hit the CALL button. The boy answered right away.

"Hello, Simon."

"Mitch? Are you okay? Ari said you hurt your head when you slid off that mountain. Man, that hole was big. Why didn't you see it?"

"Dark and rainy night. I'm doing better. I still have headaches like you did."

"Isn't it awesome that Ari got her voice back and could help you?"

While Mitch considered that the accident had been the impetus for shocking her back into speech mode, he felt thankful she hadn't been injured. "Totally. Have you talked about your parents since she got her voice back?"

"Yeah. You were right. She feels the same way I do but couldn't tell anyone."

"Keep talking to her, Simon," Mitch encouraged. "I went fishing today. Wished you were there with me."

"Cool. Did you catch the big one?"

"Not even a minnow. I suspect those big fish decided it wasn't worth showing their gills because you weren't around to catch them."

The boy chortled with laughter.

"How are you doing, Simon? Everything okay now that you're back in Chicago?"

"I want to go home, but Ari says the police won't let us. She makes me go to the office with her. Won't let me go to my friends' houses. They have to come here."

"Hang in there, buddy. Is Ari around?"

"She's on her cell phone."

"Will you tell her I called? Ask her to call me?"

"Sure. What's your number?"

She already had his number and hadn't used it in the days she'd been gone. Mitch recited his cell number to the boy. "Call me anytime you like, Simon. I want to stay in touch with you and Ari. I consider you friends. Look after her, buddy. And yourself."

"I will, Mitch."

After dinner, he cleaned the kitchen and went to pack. He'd get to bed early. Ari hadn't returned his call and Mitch doubted she would. He'd hoped she might have had a change of heart and would be willing to talk.

Had he been fair to involve Simon like that? Why hadn't he told her the truth? Because he'd known her response would have been more immediate. She would have sent him away on that first day. Those nights on the deck never would have happened because she wouldn't have bared her soul to a psychiatrist.

Why couldn't she accept that he was a flesh-and-blood man prone to mistakes? Sure, the medical degree was part of who he was, but not all. He wouldn't give up hope. Couldn't. Mitch had to believe that one day she would find forgiveness for him in her heart.

After he showered and climbed into bed, Mitch allowed his thoughts to center on the God of Ari's life.

His faith had died with his parents. Jen had been

completely different. She attended church with their aunt. His sister derived a great deal of comfort from her love of God and had shared that with him frequently over the years.

He listened out of politeness but doubted God could do anything for him personally. When Jen said she prayed for him, Mitch decided it was something she needed to do. But for some reason the idea of prayer didn't seem as alien since he'd witnessed Ari's love for the Lord. He'd searched for something ever since his parents' death. Maybe now was the time for him to find it in a relationship with God.

Mitch lay against the pillow, propping his hands behind his head as he pondered what he needed to do.

"Jesus," he said finally, "I don't know the right way to do this. I don't even know if You're listening. I sure could use Your help. Ari is angry with me. She's entitled, but please help her accept I never intended to hurt her. And Lord God, guide me. It's been too many years since I accepted You as my Savior. Years when I didn't serve You or follow my faith. Help me find my way back to You now. Please take care of Ari and Simon. Aid the police in locating their parents' killer and give them peace. Take care of my family and keep them safe. Amen."

≈

"That was Mitch. He wants you to call him at this number," Simon said, handing over the scrap of paper he'd scribbled on.

She nodded, wishing Simon would share more of their conversation. Why had Mitch called? What did he think they had to discuss? She'd ended their relationship at the hospital in Murphy.

Pain filled her at the thought. She liked Mitch. She had trusted him, made him privy to information about her life and business. He'd broken her heart with his lies.

"When, God, when will this stop?"

As a Christian, Ari knew she wasn't protected from attack.

She also knew that she had someone to turn to in times when she felt most in need of help.

She could accept that Mitch wanted to help Gary, but she couldn't deal with his hiding the truth from her. He had talked to Dwayne Graves. Mitch knew about her condition. Ari didn't want to be psychoanalyzed by anyone, particularly not by a man to whom she felt a strong attraction.

Mitch had to know how she'd feel, but he'd hidden the truth. Perhaps he felt it best, but it wasn't his call. He should have told her. Let her decide.

She and Shannon had discussed the situation yesterday at lunch. She had asked her friend to pray with her.

"You already admitted you like him. So he messed up. It's not like he tried to do something really bad to you."

"He lied. You know how I feel about that."

"No, he didn't," Shannon said. "He chose to hold back a fact that he knew would make you send him away."

"That's worse than lying. It's deceit."

"Not everyone can live up to your standards, Ari. You couldn't afford to send him away. You needed him. Have you considered that maybe it was a chance he wasn't willing to take? That he felt so strongly about being near you that he was willing to risk making you angry?"

"Maybe that wouldn't have happened if he'd told me from the beginning."

Shannon shook her head at Ari's response. "Now who's lying? He didn't tell you because he knew how you'd react."

"How could he know, Shannon? He didn't know me. He assumed I was like everyone else."

"And he wasn't wrong. Did you not behave exactly as he expected?"

To her annoyance, she felt a blush spread over her cheeks. Shannon was her friend. Why was she defending Mitch? "Why is it wrong for me to expect truth from the people I associate with?" she demanded.

"Sometimes it's best to keep things to yourself until you have a better understanding of the situation."

"Is that what you do, Shannon?"

"If you mean would I keep something that might hurt you a secret, I have to admit it's possible."

She stared.

Shannon went on. "I'd pray over the situation. Seek God's guidance and then do what I felt led to do. And anything I do would be out of love for you and with the best of intentions. There's more to trust than you think. Sometimes you have to trust a person to stand by you and do what they feel needs to be done.

"And whether you want to admit it or not, you owe Mitchell Ellis a debt you can never repay. Your feelings for him pushed you to cry out for help that night. You had to save him because no matter what he'd done, you cared. And you still care. That's why you're avoiding him."

Shannon made sense. Ari had trusted him. Hadn't he been there for her? Done his best to help her overcome her fears? Like Tom, Mitch had lost sleep to see that they were safe. He'd even provided her a safe haven to hole up in until she was able to move on. Until the accident that gave her voice back. And then she'd run away again.

She might say she wanted her life back, but she was still acting like a coward.

fourteen

"Raquel, come in," Mitch said as she entered his office. "Good to see you."

Even though he had resumed seeing patients a couple of days after returning to Chicago, this was her first appointment since his return.

"You, too, Dr. Ellis. Your service told me about your accident. I hope you're okay."

The hairline scar was barely noticeable.

"Yes," he said, more out of politeness than anything else. "I'm doing fine now. Have a seat and we'll get started. How have you been, Raquel?"

She took a seat on the sofa. "Not so good."

Mitch wondered how long they were going to dance around the truth of their last meeting. "What's wrong?"

"This situation with Ari. She won't talk to me."

Two things hit him at once. Raquel had used a name in their session. Ari's name. And she'd said Ari wouldn't have anything to do with her.

That's my girl, Mitch thought, happy to hear Ari had listened to his advice and steered clear of this woman.

Raquel continued to talk. "I wanted to be there for her and Simon, but they disappeared and no one knew where they went. Now she's had Todd removed from his position. He's devastated. He worked so hard to gain his position in the firm. But then, you already knew that. Why were you at the meeting with Ari? I didn't know you knew each other."

Mitch glanced at the folder in his lap. "Why did you call yourself Ann Radnor?"

"Why were you at the meeting?" Raquel repeated.

"I attended at Ms. Kent's request." Mitch could see that the roundabout response frustrated Raquel. "Does it bother you that she got upset over Langan's plan for Ann Radnor to take over her job?"

She didn't acknowledge the use of her alias.

"He said she asked for his help."

Not likely, Mitch thought. Evidently Mr. Langan hadn't shared his failure to make contact with Arianna. "Why wouldn't you think your action would cause her further upset at a dreadful time in her life?"

Raquel's expression turned defensive. "We wanted to help. She stopped talking and disappeared without a word. Todd said. . .Ari asked for help. I never would have agreed otherwise."

"She didn't."

Raquel became more agitated after Mitch's denial. She stood and walked the room. "I'm not so sure I should continue seeing you."

Mitch strove to appear concerned. Given what she'd done to Ari, he wasn't so sure he wanted to see her either. He forced himself to remain calm. He needed to hear what she had to say. "Why did you call yourself Ann Radnor?"

Raquel didn't answer.

"Did you attend the Kents' dinner party with your fiancé?"

"Yes," she snapped.

In their last session, she'd raged over the mistreatment she'd received at a party. "Is Charles Kent the man you've talked about all these years, Raquel? Or should I call you Ann?"

"I didn't want it to become common knowledge that I was seeing a shrink. My name is Raquel Ann Radnor. Ann is more suitable for business. Wilson is my mother's maiden name."

"Our sessions are confidential. I would never share your true identity."

"I can't be certain of that, can I, Dr. Ellis?" She turned around and eyed him for several seconds.

"You can," Mitch said with a shrug. "You said you're troubled by the Kent situation. Do you want to discuss those feelings?"

"Of course I'm troubled that someone I knew and respected was senselessly murdered. It's wrong on so many levels. And I resent being considered a suspect. I had nothing to do with their deaths."

"Are you grieving for Charles Kent, Raquel?"

"I'm thrilled Ari has her voice back. Were you working with her?"

Mitch eyed her but didn't respond.

"You are. What made her voice return?"

More shock, Mitch thought, recalling that night on the mountain. "It happens that way."

"I've called, but she refuses to take my calls."

Mine, too, Mitch thought glumly. "You don't think she's entitled to feel angry after that furtive attempt to take over her company?"

"She shouldn't be upset because we wanted to help her. I heard Ari has been appointed Simon's guardian and has complete control of her parents' shares."

Mitch watched the play of emotions on her face.

"If that's true, they should appoint someone to look after Simon's interests."

"Why would you say that?"

"He needs someone to protect him."

"Ari loves her brother. She'll make sure he never wants for anything."

Her face whitened.

"Simon has a nanny, Raquel. I recall a session where

you complained about the woman who didn't spend time with your newborn son."

She ignored his observation. "Ari does love Simon."

He nodded. "She cares more about him than herself. That makes it really hard to accept the injustice of what happened to her. Not really fair, don't you agree, Raquel?"

"Why would you ask me that?" she demanded. "I tell you I had nothing to do with what happened."

Mitch fought to control his fury toward this woman who had hurt Ari with her actions. "Do you have any idea what happened that night?"

"N–no." She stumbled over the word.

"How long have you been coming here, Raquel?"

She pointed to the folder in his lap. "You have my chart right there."

"I do. And do you consider me to be an intelligent man?"

"What do you mean?"

"Several years ago, you came to me, depressed and upset that your affair had ended and the man convinced you to give up your son for the child's sake." She refused to look at him. "You were angry, Raquel. Furious that the man you loved took your heart and your child and tossed you away without a thought."

"He didn't."

"You said he did. Why didn't you tell me you were once Charles Kent's assistant? Why would you leave such a job?"

"You have been talking to someone about me," she accused.

"I asked about Ann Radnor. Not Raquel Wilson."

"It was a step up the career ladder."

Her claim didn't ring true. "Was it, Raquel? Could a sales manager position possibly be more prestigious than assistant to the CEO of Kent Enterprises?"

"It wasn't fair," she cried out. "He said he loved me. He promised to take care of me."

Horror filled her expression as she realized the import of her revelation. She curled in a fetal position on the sofa, tears trailing along her cheeks. Her voice grew soft. "I never knew anyone like him. When we started working together, he praised and encouraged me, said he could see me going far in the business. I listened when he talked about his wife and how she never wanted more children. It broke my heart to see how sad that made him. He wanted a son. He loved Ari, but she was young and didn't show any interest in the company."

"What did you do, Raquel?"

She became defiant. "I loved him. And he loved me."

"Are you Simon Kent's mother?"

She didn't speak for several minutes, and then she nodded. "I didn't mean for it to happen. Charles didn't seem at all upset when I told him. Said we'd handle the situation. I was afraid he meant an abortion, but he wanted me to have the baby. Said if it was a son, he'd bring him into the business and make him as successful as himself. I wanted my son to have all the opportunities in life I couldn't give him. That's why I agreed to the private adoption."

"Did Michelle Kent know you were Simon's mother?"

She shook her head. "I don't know what he did, but I suspect Charles begged her forgiveness and asked her to raise my son."

"Why would he do that?" Mitch asked.

"Divorce would have taken everything he'd worked so hard for over the years."

"Did she agree to raise your child?"

"Not right away. Charles stayed in the hotel for a couple of weeks before she sent for him. He told me it would be better if we didn't see each other again and returned home. He paid my living expenses until I was able to return to work and helped me find another job. Then he said I shouldn't ever contact him again."

"And you did so willingly?"

"What else could I do?" she cried. "My son needed his father. Charles could give him so much more than I could."

"You could have loved him. You could have given him everything he needed to grow into a successful man in his own right."

"Do you think I don't regret my decision? Once I signed those papers, it was too late. I couldn't go back. Charles would have dragged me through the courts, and they would have granted him custody because he'd tell them I wasn't stable and had already given away my son. If I'd changed my mind, it would have destroyed us both."

"Why did you go to his home that night?"

Her expression grew stony, her tone cool. "I went with my fiancé. I've moved on and thought he had, too."

After the times she'd cried over the man telling her to stay out of his life, Mitch found it difficult to accept her response. He leaned more toward a need to see the man or force him to acknowledge her existence. "What did he say to hurt you?"

"He was so cold," she said almost sadly. "I complimented him on the art. We'd often visited galleries. Liked the same artists. He looked at me strangely and then invited me into the office to see his latest acquisition. I didn't know he would be so cruel. Demanded to know what game I was playing. Said I wasn't welcome in his home. I told him not to make a scene. Pointed out that he had as much to lose as I did. There was a photo of my son on his desk. I said he must be proud of this handsome boy. That's when he said he wouldn't allow me to disrupt their lives. Disrupt his life," she jeered. "His life was never disrupted. Mine was destroyed." She paused before speaking again. "Then he said, 'I'm not having this discussion. You signed the papers. Stand by your agreement and I'll stand by mine.' "

Her cheeks turned red against a pale face. "I never had any

intention of doing anything to harm my son," she declared.

"What else have you done, Raquel? Did you see Simon at church?"

Her downcast gaze provided Mitch with his answer.

"He was so precious. I volunteered in his Sunday school classrooms."

"Did Charles know?"

"I don't think so."

"Was that enough for you?"

"I tried to move on with my life. I got really depressed. That's when I came to you. Charles paid your fees. He knew my problems were his fault. But he didn't care about me. He had everything he wanted. I had nothing."

"And?"

"Then I met Todd and had this crazy idea that if I married a successful man, maybe when Simon was older, I could tell him I was his birth mother. I hoped that he wouldn't hate me for giving him up."

"Does Todd know the truth?"

Raquel sighed. "I never stopped loving Charles. No matter what he'd done to me, we shared a child. He cared for that child and in my mind that meant he cared for me. He had to love me. I'd given him a son."

"How does Todd feel about that?"

"He hated Charles. Said he loved me far more than Kent ever would. When I got really sad and cried, he said he'd make him suffer. Todd knew I'd never love him like I loved Charles, but he still wanted to marry me."

"But you never married him. It's been two years, Raquel."

She stood and walked over to the window, her back to Mitch. "I couldn't promise to love and honor Todd when another man already occupied my heart."

"The man who cast you aside? Took your child? He used you, Raquel."

She whirled around. "I'm not stupid, Dr. Ellis. I know all that in my head, but my heart told me differently."

Mitch understood the need to listen to the heart. When he'd first met Ari, his intention had been to protect her, but somewhere along the way that intention had shifted to something far different. He still needed to protect her, but his feelings for her were much stronger.

"Ari doesn't know."

Raquel shook her head. "It was between Charles and me."

"Does Langan know the entire story?"

"Most of it."

"Why was he so determined to find Ari when she and Simon disappeared?"

"What do you mean?" Raquel demanded.

"What about the board?" Mitch asked. "Was the attempted takeover his idea?"

"Todd never said anything about a takeover."

"Did he plan to use you to take control of the board?"

She covered her mouth as the realization hit. "He did it all for me."

"And Simon."

She nodded slowly. "When I came back into the room, he could see that I was upset. He demanded to know what had happened. He said we'd get Simon back. Raise him together."

"Did you believe him?"

She shook her head. "It was too late. I wasn't about to rob Simon of the only security he knew, no matter how much I wanted to be part of his life. Todd was furious when I refused. I said I'd never speak to him again if he didn't leave it alone."

"What did he do, Raquel?"

"Nothing."

Dawning realization suddenly filled her expression. "You think he. . . No. He wouldn't."

Suddenly she grabbed her purse and ran toward the door.

Mitch hurried after her. "Raquel? Come back."

She was gone. He grabbed the phone and dialed. "Who's the detective for the Kent case?" he demanded when Gary answered.

"Mitch? What's going on?"

"Call him now. Tell him to look into Todd Langan as a person of interest."

"Why? What do you know, Mitch?"

"I can't tell you, Gary. Make sure Ari and Simon are safe. I have a feeling something bad is about to happen."

Mitch disconnected and dialed Ari's cell number, planning to leave a message. She surprised him by answering the phone. "Where are you?"

There was a slight pause, and then she said, "At home. Simon has the flu."

"Don't leave the house. Get Tom inside and lock up tight. I'll be there in a few minutes to explain."

"But Simon has a doctor's appointment in an hour."

"Please, Arianna. I'll take care of everything. Promise me you'll stay there."

Mitch held the phone to his ear as he ran upstairs. He removed the pouch from the nightstand drawer, sliding out the gun and clip. "And whatever you do, stay away from Todd Langan and Raquel. . .I mean Ann Radnor."

"Todd called a few minutes ago," she said. "He wanted to come by and discuss my decision not to work with him. I told him Simon has an appointment. I really don't want to deal with him. I'll ask Erik George to—"

"Stay away from Todd Langan," Mitch interrupted. "I don't have all the facts, but I'm fairly certain he's involved in your parents' murder."

She gasped and cried, "No, Mitch. You're wrong. He wouldn't do that."

"You have no idea what Langan can do. Please trust me."

"Tell me why I should trust you."

Her plea touched that part of him that knew he had to be honest if he ever hoped to have a future with her. She wouldn't accept anything less from him. "Sometimes I hear things. I shouldn't tell you. It involves a patient. Someone you know. This is bad, Ari. Please believe me."

"Okay, I'll call Dr. Graves and cancel the appointment."

Relieved, he promised, "I'll tell you everything. The minute I get there. Stay safe."

Mitch ran downstairs and locked up the house, going out through the kitchen door into the garage.

His cell rang as he got into his car. "Mitch, Gary here. The detective says they already have Langan as a person of interest."

He hit the gas, barely waiting for the garage door to clear. "He called her, Gary. Wanted to come by to discuss the reason she won't continue working with him. She told him Simon had a doctor's appointment."

"You think he's at the townhouse?"

"I'd say he's fairly close. He's not stable. She promised to stay put, but you know Ari."

"I'll call Tom. Where are you?"

"In my car. Hold on. Something's not right." He climbed out of the car and fought back his anger. Why now of all the times in the world? "My tire's flat."

"Want me to send someone over?"

"No!" he shouted. "Keep Ari safe. I'll call a cab. See you soon."

"Okay, calm down. More men are on the way. We'll surround the place. I'll tie her to a chair if I have to."

"Do whatever you have to do to keep her safe."

fifteen

Mitch exited the cab and surveyed the police presence in the neighborhood. He tried to ask questions, but an officer instructed him to move on.

"He's with me," Gary called as he exited the building. The officer shrugged and turned his attention back to crowd control.

"What happened?" Mitch demanded. Thanks to the flat tire and an accident that blocked a major intersection, it had been well over an hour since he talked with Ari. He'd tried to call and gotten her voice mail.

"Tom came down to check the perimeter and spotted Langan's silver sports car parked over there." Gary pointed to the far end of the street. The car was still there. "The idiot was watching the townhouse through a rifle scope."

"A rifle. . ." Mitch broke off and Gary nodded.

"You don't think he planned. . ." Mitch shuddered at the thought of what might have happened if Ari and Simon had left the house. "Where's Ari? Is she okay?"

"Tom called the police. They found a high-powered rifle in the car. At first he tried to pretend he was concerned for their safety but they already had the story. Ann Radnor called the police. Evidently she convinced them Langan was a danger to Ari. Then she called Todd and broke off their engagement."

"Gary, answer me. Is she okay?" Mitch demanded.

"They're both fine. I've got so many men in that condo Langan couldn't have found her if he'd gotten inside."

Mitch wanted to know everything, but he needed to see Ari. Needed to keep his promise.

"The police arrested the man who killed the Kents three

days ago. He was in a bar bragging about killing those rich people. He said their attorney had paid him well for the job.

"Even told how Langan let him into the penthouse the night of the dinner party. He hid out until everyone was gone. Said Langan made his job easier by drugging the Kents. The man has a rap sheet as long as your arm. Likes knives. Hurt his girlfriend pretty badly when she tried to get away from him. She lived to tell the story."

"But Ari. The gun." Mitch couldn't formulate a complete sentence if his life depended on his doing so.

"Langan told them everything. He's obsessed with Ann Radnor and hated Charles Kent. He promised to get her child back and believed that would convince her he loved her more than Kent ever had. When everything started falling apart, he decided to kill Ari so Ann could get Simon back. He must have been desperate to come here himself."

"Does Ari know?"

"The detective is with her now."

He couldn't bear another minute of this. "I've got to get up there, Gary."

"Come on. I'll get you in."

Mitch paused and grimaced. "Simon has the flu. I promised Ari I'd take care of him."

"Go see Ari. I'll call Dr. Graves and ask him to call in a prescription."

"Thanks, buddy. I owe you one."

"Nah, we'll call it even. You sent me the love of my life. Why shouldn't I return the favor? Ari's over there," he said, indicating the sofa, "with the police."

"Mitch," Ari called the moment she spotted him. She held out her hand.

He hurried over and sat next to her on the sofa. Taking her trembling hand in his, he asked, "Are you okay?"

"Todd. . . Did you hear?" Her gaze met his.

He nodded. The detective sat on the chair opposite them.

"Will you stay?"

Mitch tightened his hold on her hand. Nothing short of dynamite was going to move him from her side.

The detective flipped his pad open. "Todd Langan has admitted to contracting the murder of your parents."

"Todd?" Ari's voice broke slightly.

"Yes, ma'am."

"No!" Ari's keening wail broke Mitch's heart. She clutched his arm. "It can't be. Why would he do that?" She stared at the detective.

"I'm sorry, Ms. Kent," the man began, unable to disguise his discomfort. "Ann Radnor contacted us about Langan. She informed us of her involvement with your father."

Ari's mouth dropped open.

"Langan's obsession pushed him to eliminate your father from the picture."

"My father?"

"He believed that if he eliminated you and your parents, they could regain custody of the child. Your brother."

"Simon?"

He nodded. "Ann Radnor is Simon's mother."

"No." Ari's head moved from side to side. "He's my brother."

"Charles Kent is his father."

Ari's eyes closed and she breathed deeply, her distress evident. "What are you saying?"

Mitch slipped an arm around Ari's shoulder and pulled her close.

"Langan believed the estate would go to Simon as the last remaining Kent heir. We think he planned to help Ann regain custody of her son and take control of the company."

"But surely he knew he would get caught." Ari turned her head into Mitch's shoulder. "He had my parents killed out of unrequited love?"

She sobbed softly, her tears wetting his neck. Mitch rubbed his hand gently across her shoulders. "It's over, Ari. He's been arrested."

She jerked up, her face pale. "It's only the beginning, Mitch. This will go to court. The media will be all over us. How do you think Simon will handle learning his birth mother's boyfriend had his parents killed?"

He squeezed her hand in his. "I'll help him work through this. Ann has no rights. You're his guardian."

"Poor Simon. He's so sick. This will make things worse."

She couldn't bear seeing this small child who meant so much to her harmed. Mitch couldn't either. "We'll protect him, Ari. If we have to move to the ends of the earth to keep him safe, that's what we'll do. No one is going to hurt him. Let's go check on him now," Mitch suggested. He looked at the detective and asked, "Can we continue this later? I need to check on my patient."

The man nodded. "We can talk later."

"Thank you," Ari said.

Together they walked down the hall to Simon's bedroom. The boy slept fitfully, the bedcovers hanging over the edge of the bed. She pulled the sheet and blanket back over him.

Mitch sat on the edge of the bed and touched Simon's forehead. "Have you given him anything for the fever?"

She nodded. "It's not helping."

"Mitch?" Simon mumbled as he came awake.

"Hey, buddy, how are you feeling?"

"Lousy."

"Let's see what we can do to make you feel better. Have you eaten today?"

"Not hungry."

"You need to eat. How about some soup and crackers? Or a Popsicle. Think you could eat that?"

"I'll try. I heard people talking. Who's here, Ari?"

"Security," she said, unwilling to upset him further. "Here, take a couple of sips of juice."

Mitch supported Simon against his chest as he sipped through the straw and then laid him back on the bed. He tucked the covers securely about him. "Go back to sleep. We'll get your medications and food."

"Okay," he mumbled weakly.

They turned out the light and stepped into the hallway, closing the door behind them.

"Do you think I should call Dr. Graves?"

Mitch grinned. "Don't you trust me? I went to medical school, too, you know."

She leaned lightly into him, tilting her face toward his. "I trust you, Mitch."

Relief greater than he could have imagined filled him. "Thank you, Ari. I've been so afraid you wouldn't ever trust me again."

"Why didn't you tell me?"

"I wanted to be there for you and Simon. You wouldn't have let me stay if you'd known the truth."

"And you can't tell me what you know?"

He shook his head. "You're smart, though. You'll put it all together."

The shock held her immobile. "I don't want to think about it. I want to close my eyes and wake up to find things like they were not so long ago. I want my parents back."

The tears came in earnest. He pulled her into his arms, his hands smoothing her shoulder. "I know, honey. But you can't go back. You have to move forward. For yourself and for Simon."

"Will you help us?"

"You know I will. I'll be there every step of the way." He cupped her face in his hand and kissed her. "I love you, Ari."

She nodded, brushing her hand along his jaw. "I love you, too."

sixteen

As Ari predicted, the next few days were a paparazzi nightmare. She depended on the security staff to fight them off and did everything in her power to keep the truth from Simon.

Ann Radnor called often, and Ari refused to talk to her. Every voice mail message was a plea for forgiveness and a request to know how Simon was holding up under the siege of the press.

While Ari knew it was her Christian duty to forgive, she found it difficult to do so. She'd prayed and asked God to help her find forgiveness for their father and the woman who had brought so much harm to her family.

Healthwise, things were looking up for Simon. He recovered from the flu and just the day before had his cast removed. Ari needed to talk to her brother and didn't feel she could face this alone. Remembering Mitch's promise, she called to request his help.

"You're sure you want to do this now?"

"I have to. It's all over the news. What happens if he reads about it on the Internet or hears from someone else? He'll be upset that I didn't tell him the truth."

"Around seven thirty tonight?"

"Thanks, Mitch. Come for dinner."

≥∙

He arrived right on time. Dora Etheridge had returned to Ari's that afternoon after Ari called to tell her what they planned to do. Ari prepared Simon's favorites. The dining table had been set with place mats and everyday china. A huge bowl of spaghetti sat in the middle along with cheese bread.

Ari led the way, indicating Mitch should sit next to her. Simon sat across from Ari, with Nana next to him.

He sensed Ari's internal struggle over what she had to do. Reaching over, Mitch squeezed her hand in his and whispered, "It's going to be okay, Ari. Simon knows you love him."

Her gaze focused on him for a long time before she answered, "It's so hard, Mitch. No child should have to deal with something like this."

"We'll work it out," he promised. "Let's pray." Taking her hand and Simon's, he waited for them to bring Nana into the circle before he blessed the food and asked for God's guidance.

After dinner they went into the family room. Ari asked Nana to join the group.

"Simon, I have something to tell you."

The boy looked from one adult to another and then back to Ari. "That I'm adopted?"

Shocked, she demanded, "Who told you?"

"This guy at school likes to pick on the little kids. He heard it on the news and texted me."

Mitch witnessed her despair, saw the way her eyes drifted closed. Knew she blamed herself for not acting quickly enough. How could he help her fix this?

Simon stood and came over to wrap his arms around her neck. "It's okay, Ari."

Her arms tightened. "Oh Simon. Why didn't you tell me?"

"I wanted to, but I was afraid."

Tears leaked from Ari's eyes and trailed along her cheeks. The sins of the father had come to bear on this small brave boy. "I love you, Simon. Please don't ever be afraid to talk to me."

"I love you, too, Ari. I'm glad you're my sister."

"I am, you know. Dad is your father, too."

Simon rested against Ari. "I miss Mom and Dad."

"Me, too," Ari told him. "But we're family, Simon. You and me. You can always trust me to be there for you. I want to see you grow up healthy and happy. I want you to tell me everything. I'll be there lots of times when you'll wish I weren't."

"I'd never wish that," Simon said, a mischievous grin touching his face as he added, "You're my favorite sister."

"Rascal," she said, tickling him before she said with an affected tone, "I'm your only sistah."

The boy laughed and she hugged him.

"We're a team, Simon. No matter what happens in the future, it's you and me."

"Is Ms. Ann my mom? That's what Tony said."

Mitch wanted to have a chat with this bully.

"He said they called it a love triangle. Said Mr. Langan had Mom and Dad killed because Ms. Ann was in love with Dad. They said Mr. Langan wanted her to have her son back. Did he really do that?"

Mitch glanced at Ari and back to Simon. "Yes, that's true."

"Am I going to have to live with her now?"

Horrified, Ari exclaimed, "No. Never. You're staying right here with me."

A frown carved its mark on Simon's forehead. "But what if Ms. Ann wants me back?"

"She can't have you. We're family, Simon. Ann gave up her rights. One day when you're older, you may decide you want to have a relationship with her. When that time comes, we'll consider it, but for now she has a lot of personal issues to work through and won't be involved in your life."

"Where is she?"

"She left Chicago."

"Do you know where she went?"

Ari shook her head. "I haven't talked to her."

"You're mad at her, aren't you?"

This child was too perceptive for his own good.

"Yes, I'm angry with a lot of people for what they've done. They were adults, Simon. They should have known better."

"We need to pray that God will come into their lives and change them like He changed us."

"Yes, sweetheart, we do." Ari hugged him close for several seconds.

"If you ever want to talk about this, I'm there for you," Mitch said.

"Thanks, Mitch, but if you don't mind, I think I'll talk to Jesus first."

Mitch bumped fists with the boy. "I think that's a pretty smart thing to do."

"You do?"

He nodded. "I accepted Jesus into my heart when I was eleven years old, but then my parents died in a fire, and I didn't talk to Him after that. I thought I was a smart guy, but I wasn't really."

Simon smiled proudly at his sister. "Ari introduced me to God."

"And you and Ari reintroduced me to Him. You're disciples, Simon. You lead people to Jesus and He does the rest."

"That's awesome."

Mitch grinned at the boy's response. "Jesus is awesome. I want to get to know Him better than I did when I was eleven. And now that Ari is talking again and can go to Bible study, I'm hoping she'll invite me."

Simon glanced at his sister.

She smiled at Mitch. "Anytime you want."

Mitch winked at her. "Are you okay with all this, Simon?"

"I don't understand everything. Mom and Dad shouldn't have been killed like that. Killing is wrong. It's a commandment. Like those ones we saw written on the mountain."

"Yes," Ari agreed. She could have told him there was another commandment regarding adultery. "I want you to promise that when you hear things you find confusing, you'll come to me and ask questions. I'll tell you the truth. And when people say hurtful things, I need you to talk to me about what they said."

"Do what Ari says, Simon. Don't think you're being brave when you bottle it up inside."

"But Dad always said real men don't cry like babies."

"Real men are human," Mitch declared. "They hurt and that hurt needs an outlet. Maybe your dad believed he had to be tough to earn respect."

He looked at Ari and then back at Simon, trying to gauge how to continue. He hadn't known their father and what drove him.

"It's good to talk to adults about the things that bother you. Sometimes when you talk problems out, you realize they really aren't that important in the first place."

"Okay. Can I go watch my show now?"

Ari smiled and nodded her permission. The boy darted away to his bedroom.

Nana rose to follow. "I'll check on him."

Mitch knew she wanted to give them some privacy. "Simon will be fine. He knows you love him," he told Ari.

"Thanks for being here, Mitch." She looked at him, her eyes filled with a deep, curious longing.

Her tender regard was his undoing. "I realize we haven't known each other that long, but I love you. I'd like it if we could spend more time together. Get to know each other. I love the sound of your voice, but I loved you when you couldn't utter a word. I want to hear that voice every day for the rest of my life."

A cheeky smile flashed on Ari's face. "Are you asking for a date, Dr. Ellis?"

Mitch grinned in return. "More than one, Ms. Kent."

"Good. I'm ready to take this first step of the journey to learn God's plan for our future."

"Me, too," he agreed, cupping her face in his hands and kissing her softly.

The sweet kiss filled her heart with joy. Ari smiled at him, her gaze holding his as she sent up a silent thank-you to God.

A Letter To Our Readers

Dear Reader:

In order that we might better contribute to your reading enjoyment, we would appreciate your taking a few minutes to respond to the following questions. We welcome your comments and read each form and letter we receive. When completed, please return to the following:

Fiction Editor
Heartsong Presents
PO Box 719
Uhrichsville, Ohio 44683

1. Did you enjoy reading *With Not a Spoken Word* by Terry Fowler?
   ❑ Very much! I would like to see more books by this author!
   ❑ Moderately. I would have enjoyed it more if

   _____

   _____

   _____

2. Are you a member of **Heartsong Presents**? ❑ Yes ❑ No
   If no, where did you purchase this book? _____

   _____

3. How would you rate, on a scale from 1 (poor) to 5 (superior), the cover design? _____

4. On a scale from 1 (poor) to 10 (superior), please rate the following elements.

   ____ Heroine   ____ Plot
   ____ Hero   ____ Inspirational theme
   ____ Setting   ____ Secondary characters

5. These characters were special because? _____

_____

_____

6. How has this book inspired your life? _____

_____

_____

7. What settings would you like to see covered in future
   Heartsong Presents books? _____

_____

_____

8. What are some inspirational themes you would like to see
   treated in future books? _____

_____

_____

9. Would you be interested in reading other **Heartsong
   Presents** titles? ❏ Yes ❏ No

10. Please check your age range:
    ❏ Under 18   ❏ 18-24
    ❏ 25-34   ❏ 35-45
    ❏ 46-55   ❏ Over 55

Name _____

Occupation _____

Address _____

City, State, Zip _____

E-mail _____

KENTUCKY WEDDINGS

The three Truelove siblings of Paris, Kentucky, find that God answers prayers in the most unlikely packages that are wrapped in love.

Contemporary, paperback, 368 pages, 5.1875" x 8"

Please send me ____ copies of *Kentucky Weddings*. I am enclosing $7.99 for each. (Please add $4.00 to cover postage and handling per order. OH add 7% tax. If outside the U.S. please call 740-922-7280 for shipping charges.)

Name _____

Address _____

City, State, Zip_____

To place a credit card order, call 1-740-922-7280.
Send to: Heartsong Presents Readers' Service, PO Box 721, Uhrichsville, OH 44683

Heartsong

Presents

Great Inspirational Romance
at a Great Price!

Heartsong Presents books are inspirational romances in contemporary and historical settings, designed to give you an enjoyable, spirit-lifting reading experience. You can choose wonderfully written titles from some of today's best authors like Wanda E. Brunstetter, Mary Connealy, Susan Page Davis, Cathy Marie Hake, Joyce Livingston, and many others.

When ordering quantities less than six, above titles are $3.99 each.
Not all titles may be available at time of order.